A Strand of Your Love

"I dedicate this novel to those who doubted me
and to those who believed in me.
For every journey begins with a single step,
even if it must be taken against the wind.
Thank you — it is thanks to you that this story came to be."

— Zuzanna Ziętarska

Chapter 1

The Life I Learned to Endure

"Please come in, Alice," says the boss. I clutch the white wooden door handle so tightly that it digs into my hand like tiny needles. I rely on my courage and peek into the office of my company's director.

"You wanted to see me, Mr. Moyer. I came as quickly as I could," the empty sound of the keyboard on his computer stifles my stressed thoughts. Is he going to fire me? Or perhaps he just wants to ask about other employees.

Hello. You probably have no idea why you're here. I warn you, I have no ill intentions, but I must treat every matter the same. React. It's about the well-being and, I admit, the reputation of our company," his voice suddenly seems so terrifying and piercing that I swallow loudly. "I understand," I respond, as heavily as possible.

"Alice, one of your coworkers told me this isn't the first time you've come to work not in the best condition. I know you're a good worker, you try your best. But I hope you understand why I must react," he says with difficulty.

"Yes, I understand. However, I have no clue what you're talking about," I respond, feigning disbelief. I know very well what my boss, standing in front of me face to face, wants to convey. I am fully aware of the state I come to work in and how hard it is to maintain an insincere smile on my face.

"You've been working here for a while now," he continues. "And, that's why I invited you here." As Moyer speaks these words, suddenly all my words run out. Suddenly, I, a chatty reader of teen magazines, don't know what to say.

"Mr. Moyer, I'm not used to discussing my personal life with my boss. And I think the problems that my coworker noticed have just such a basis," I say in a quiet voice. "I understand, I understand," he continues, but he's not convincing me.

"Do you know I have a small child at home?" I add, breaking through the five-minute silence. "Yes, it can't be overlooked. Many times you've been late or haven't come to work because of your child's illness." I understand all, it seems to me that honesty isn't his strong suit.

"Why did you want to see me? Please be specific," I add. "I'll tell you straight. You're a good worker, but if you don't stop coming to work unkempt and bruised, I'll have to fire you or move you to the kitchen. I don't want to be malicious, but I must do something about such a problem."

His words make no impression on me. He isn't the first person who judges me from above and isn't the first person who judges me without knowing me or my life at all. However, as is appropriate for me in my situation, I respond calmly. "Of course, I understand you, sir. I'll improve, please give me a week. Goodbye." I leave my boss's office so quickly that I didn't even notice the receptionists who were waving at me with a nice smile. What the hell am I supposed to do now?

The day drags on relentlessly. Adam has a fever again. Even though I know what to do, I feel as helpless as if I had just given birth to him today. The clock strikes four in the afternoon. I have about twenty-four minutes of peace left. I don't know whether to start eating lunch, tend to my son, or hang the laundry.

When Olaf returns, the whole day's plan will unfortunately fall apart. I ask myself the same question every day. What am I doing here? When Olaf comes home, he does exactly what I've seen every day since we met. The difference is that back then, I was deeply in love and believed every promise, every kind look, every sweet kiss. I'm here, he shouts from the hall-way, bumping into the frames hanging on the wall with pictures of my parents. I know this kind of greeting. As always, he's had a few beers.

Of course, I don't respond. I take Adam from the living room and head towards the bedroom. In vain, he catches me in the hallway. "Aren't you going to say hello, baby girl?" he laughs, exhaling every percent of alcohol in his system onto me. I push through his heavy arms with my son in my arms. "Is it so hard to say hello?" he adds.

"Leave me alone." I reflexively cover up. I shield my child's face and shoulders with my elbow so that he wouldn't get hurt like last time. I understand that my son is only a year old and that no significant touch should harm him. However, I prefer to be cautious.

"Say hello. I got a promotion, you can put him to bed and pour a beer." He doesn't even pronounce his name aloud. I hear him when I've managed to get past his arms. I put Adam into the crib, each time in such situations I do it more gently. I want to compensate for what he hears, even though I know he doesn't yet understand what's happening around him. I move towards the living room. Once again, I pass the pictures of my parents. I see the gold and white curtains moving as if to the rhythm of music, letting a lot of air into the apartment. In the past, I used to close the window to not let too many mosquitoes in. My son likes to scratch the marks off his skin.

I hear "How long must I wait for you?, shouted   from the living room that I haven't managed to reach yet. "You have two minutes, otherwise you're sleeping outside." Finally, we reach the kitchen. I open the fridge and pour a beer into a mug with a calm movement. To this day, I don't understand who could want a beer at this hour. However, Olaf always does. After a moment, I feel a strong hit on the back of my head. I don't think about what I did to deserve it, but, rather, whether my son has woken up.

I try to apologize when I hear his yell from behind me. "How long can it take to pour a beer into a mug, you slut?" "Sorry," the only word I can manage to get out. The only one that I feel saves me. Or at least that's what I tell myself. After the daily incident, I go into the living room, placing the glass mug on a small wooden table. I feel at least embarrassed that, once again, I didn't manage to satisfy my partner's needs in time.

My mother always told me love stories before bedtime. To me, love looked like a clean sheet of paper on which lovers would write their beautiful emotions, memories, and experiences. Love was something ephemeral yet certain. Now, I've realized it doesn't hold true for me. Every day for the past five years, I've wondered why I still believe in this concept of love that my mother instilled in me. For me, love has become only a memory and pain.

Olaf wasn't always like this. He didn't always treat me poorly or humiliate me in every possible situation. We actually met at a bar by the highway where he had just finished his shift, but I thought there was no rule about where you might meet your great love. Unfortunately, I was disappointed by the family tales. My love turned out to be completely different. "Good day. I'll have a beer with raspberry juice,"

I heard a heavy voice from behind the counter stretching towards the bathrooms. Raspberry or strawberry, the man raised his voice trying to be heard over the other bar patrons. I really have no idea why this man intrigued me so much; it seems that by nature, I attract only weird and difficult people. "And you, baby girl. What are you drinking?" a young man, about 35, just offered me a drink.
At least, that's the question I asked myself in my head.
Sure! I don't know why I haven't ordered anything yet, I have no idea why I allowed myself to wait so long for Emily here in this bar, why her love affairs are so important to me. She's not my closest friend, yet I can never refuse to help her.

"Where are you from?" the stranger asked, sizing me up with his dark eyes. His brown-gold gaze penetrated my skin like an arrow. I felt uneasy but also curious why this man was interested in me today, of all days. Usually, no one shows me more interest than letting me cut in line at the train station bathroom. "I live nearby, waiting for a friend who I think won't show up," I said, instantly regretting that I had sold myself short. Sitting here alone in a gloomy place with a bar brimming with lustful young and old men. "I think I need to wait for her a little longer," I added. I'm not one of the most open people. Maybe that's why I get so nervous and start talking more when a stranger strikes up a conversation.

Unfortunately, the whole affair ended quite badly. Emily never showed up, and I was left alone with the young man at the bar. Olaf was very talkative. He told me about his travels, and I just opened my mouth in amazement. Now, much later, I know he has a good tactic. The more he lied, the more he attracted people. He never spent a month in Bali nor fought bears in Alaska, which of course, I found out after three years into our relationship when he hit me while his friend was over. He boasted from another room about how he had fooled me with his stories.

At first, everything was colorful. The flowers he brought me were colorful. His messages were colorful, and his kisses seemed endless to me. It all lasted too briefly to be true. I believed that someone saw in me something more than just a lonely orphan whose parents died in a car accident. I believed that someone wanted to be by my side when things were bad and when they were good. Unfortunately, besides being the most talkative 28-year-old in the world, I'm also the most naive.

Chapter 2

A Day That Never Ends

Like every other day, I walked six kilometers to get to work. At this early hour, there's no chance of catching a bus. Not much has changed since yesterday. The hotel rooms look no worse than yesterday, nor do I expect them to look any better tomorrow.

The hotel where I work is located less than five minutes on foot from the bus stop, I need to reach to go home. From a distance,   I see several people waiting under the shelter of the bus stop. It doesn't seem like wearing a hoodie is a good idea on such a hot day, but I have no other choice. The bruise from yesterday is more visible than I thought. It's quite large, silvery, and emerges from beneath the line of my dark hair. I persistently try to cover up every small proof that something is wrong at home. I rush to the spot as fast as my legs can carry me; my bus is just arriving.

"Hello, Alice," a quiet whisper doesn't escape me the moment I managed to press the open button on the door of my transport. "Hi," I reply without thinking. I thought it was another joke by the young people neighboring my workplace. They know me well; I'm familiar with such pranks. However, after getting on the bus, I turn around and see a man taller than me. My expression was at least surprised. "How do you know my name?" I ask indignantly. "And why are you bothering me?" I add. "Your name is on your sweatshirt. I was struck by your appearance and decided to strike up a conversation," the man said and then disappeared into the crowd of people jostling between the elderly inside the bus. He had pale skin, a vacant look, and a slight style. His hairstyle was somewhat reminiscent of a young hippie but also a character from the eighties. Blond strands fell over his slightly hunched back, and his blue eyes seemed to analyze every speck of dust in the dusty bus. His shoulders were about two meters wide, and I could have placed a glass of prosecco on his chest. Behind him wafted the scent of perfume. It was not an ordinary scent. One might think someone had just spilled a peach-lemonade shake on him. Fresh and sweet smell. I hadn't seen such an interesting face in a long time. I hadn't seen such an attractive man in a long time, well, apart from on adult reality shows after midnight. All afternoon, I wondered what exactly the stranger wanted from me. I'm not one for simple situations, so this situation required a bit of overthinking. Or maybe I'm exaggerating?

I don't know how much time passed until I reached the nursery by a dirt road where Adam was waiting for me. The bus route is always easy, of course, but on foot, I no longer have the strength. There is nothing in this world that brings me as much joy as the sight of my wonderful son. I know I can't rejoice in who his father is or what a great family we are, but I have no doubts about my child. He is a wonderful little boy. Every day I look at him and know that he will be like me, like his mom. Right now, there is nothing more beautiful than his smile and his gaze first thing in the morning upon waking. Every evening, I apologize to him for the situation we are in and how much I am unable to change our circumstances.

I don't have much time to think about how and when to escape, but I promise him that one day I will do it for him. Even if I have to give up everything. I have nothing to lose. I just need to find the right moment. I have wanted to leave Olaf for a long time, but he won't let me. I don't want to expose my child to such emotions, to such great trauma, so I keep the thought of escape deep in my pocket. Just for me and for Adam. That day will come; I don't know when yet, but every day I feel like it might be today.

On Thursday morning, I couldn't get out of bed. I don't know if it was due to exhaustion or a lack of desire to start another day. Before Adam wakes up, I rush to the kitchen to brew a cup of coffee; after all, I still have a few hours left. My watch shows 6:30, so theoretically, I have about half an hour to tidy up my hair, drink my coffee, and apply some mascara to my dark lashes. I am not one of those women who prioritize their appearance these days, but I still need to present myself decently at work and at my son's nursery.

Time flies, and I can't manage to style my hair in a sensible way. I settle for tying it in a loose bun. I'm finishing my last sip of coffee when my free time comes to an end. I greet my child with a smile, just as he greets me. I change him from his blue pajamas with white elephants into a gray tracksuit with black stripes. It's just another day.

On my way back from work, I wonder if summer is starting or if it's just my impression. The days have grown longer and the mornings warmer; I've barely noticed.

Every morning, I pass a park with a small playground for children, where everything has also brightened up. The bus is late, and I've been standing here for a while. Doesn't the lady know if the bus is coming today? It should! What's with these constant problems with public transport? I have the same issue nearly every day. A redheaded woman, in her fifties, starts talking to me. I didn't even have time to think of a response when we noticed the bus approaching. "At last!" the kind lady adds.

Before I could adjust the strap of my large leather bag, I feel the keys I was holding drop loudly onto the pavement between me and the woman standing next to me. As I begin to bend down to pick them up, I notice someone has already beaten me to it. "Hello again," says the man's voice. "Here are your keys, Alice." "Thank you," I reply in a quiet, heavy voice.

I don't know why I sometimes struggle to respond to a stranger in a normal way so that I can be heard clearly. It seems I have trouble producing the right normal sound. It's the same man who approached me here yesterday. He looks exactly like when I first saw him, with nothing changed except the color of his shirt.

Chapter 3

The Man at the Bus Stop

With a swift motion, I toss the keys into my bag. "Coming from work? The weather is quite nice today," the man begins. "Yes, I'm coming from work. Why do you ask?" At that moment, I realized I had no idea why I had asked such a question. Why am I even talking to a stranger before getting on the bus? I'm sorry for striking up a conversation. But it seems we'll often see each other here. "Why not exchange a few words to brighten the mood?" he suggests with a smile, his gaze following me.

The tall blonde reminds me of someone, but I can't quite recall who. I immediately notice his intriguing gaze. His blue eyes are complemented by very long blond lashes. When he looks at me, it feels like he sees me every day. There's nothing unfamiliar in his gaze; it's as if he has known me forever. That's how he looks at me. Why should I talk to a stranger on the bus ride home? Maybe someone is waiting for me there? "Really, please don't hit on me." What am I saying? "Hit on you? I just wanted to be nice. I don't want to be pushy, but it seems like it's been a long time since anyone was nice to you, judging by your reaction", he continues and smiles again, this time showing his teeth.He has a very sincere and broad smile. I'd be lying if I said he isn't attractive and doesn't catch the eye. Darn, I shouldn't think about a stranger this way. But well, the guy is attractive, trying to be nice, and only asked about the weather. Alice, get a grip. Don't overthink it.

"I'm very sorry. You're right. Maybe another time you'll catch me on one of my better days," I end the conversation and rush out of the bus. I don't look back, but I hear the doors close behind me and shortly after, the engine starts. Phew. What a relief to have this whole journey behind me.

It might sound strange, but the next morning, I immediately thought of the nice stranger from the previous day. I'm a bit terrified that I even entertained the thought of fantasizing about him. By fantasizing, I mean an evening at the cinema or a restaurant. Given the situation I'm in and the world I live in, such things are mere fantasies. I haven't left the apartment in years. Olaf doesn't take me out on dates. Friends have other things on their minds, and I certainly can't organize a nice evening for myself. Unless organizing clothes in the closet or polishing the glass in the living room counts as a nice evening. Only now, as I think about this, do I realize how sad my life sometimes is. I don't know what I would do without Adam. He brightens my days. He adds color to them.
Will I meet this man of fantasy again today?

As I leave work, I find myself wondering what will happen on my way home today. What emotions! I know that ninety-five percent of women in my situation would have forgotten about an encounter with a stranger an hour after it happened. But not me. I've always had a penchant for the strange, unexplained, and intriguing. That's why I feel so excited. I'm just reaching the bus stop. I look around, even though I know I shouldn't. It feels like the minutes are stretching into infinity. What am I actually waiting for? What do I expect? After all, it was just a nice man, older than me, who asked me a simple question. He said something about the weather and handed me my keys. Maybe he was right. It's been a long time since anyone was nice to me. I can't remember the last time Olaf handed me a cup of tea or even a bathroom towel when I forgot to bring a new one from the cabinet.

"Good morning, the weather is lovely again today." I could get used to this, I muse, wondering whom I inherited my odd quirks from. I dodge answers every time someone asks me something. I've always been a bit tactless but today. I don't know why I spoke up first.

He stood before me with an umbrella in black and blue polka dots. His hairstyle was the same, and his smile unchanged... I only noticed a difference in the shade of his undershirt.

"Good morning. Do I see a hint of color on your face?" the stranger responded. "Yes, the weather is nice. You're right," he added. "I wanted to ask if you've started following me. Or is this just another coincidence? Sorry for being so informal so soon. I guess that's just how I am," I continued. "Hmm, following you? Of course not. I think I could find a better occupation for a Thursday afternoon. I don't want to scare you," he replied. "You already know me," I say and extend my hand. "Alice. Hello".

The man stands before me with a somewhat embarrassed expression. He quickly adjusts his hair, sweeping the falling strands back to the crown of his head, where they belong. Yet the hair falls again onto his smooth forehead and nose. I wonder how soft they must be that they don't tickle his nose. After a moment of thought, he takes my hand. His skin is so delicate yet his grip is so strong. Decisive. I don't feel his fingerprints, but I feel as though I can sense every muscle in his body through his grip alone. Never in my life have I had so many thoughts about someone's handshake.

"I'm Max. I'm not a detective," he replies, anticipating my question before I ask it. He smiles again and adjusts his hairstyle. "But no, I'm not here by accident," he adds. Suddenly, I felt slightly scared. If he's neither a detective nor following me, I have no other idea who this man might actually be. This man, whose name I now know, Max. I don't understand. Not by accident? "Can you explain?" I don't know why I said that with a slight smile on my face. "Alice, I remember you from the hotel where you work," he suddenly dropped a bombshell.

Chapter 4

What He Knew

What, please? What on earth is he talking about? I suddenly thought that this might be worse than him not being a detective. He hadn't followed me, but that's exactly how I felt, as if he had. I think my face turned as pale as a wall, my mouth dry, and my hands felt almost bloodless, as if they weren't properly supplied with blood. "What's happening here? How so"? I added after a good five minutes of silence.

"I once stayed at that hotel and overheard your conversation with the boss. I didn't mean to eavesdrop. You were speaking quite loudly. I passed you several times in the hallway, but your facial expression told me everything. I didn't need to ask if something had happened or if I could help in any way. Unfortunately, I didn't ask then, but I think that was the help you needed." I don't understand why he suddenly became more talkative. I'm talking to him again but this is the first time he's told me so many things in one sentence. I don't know if it's shock or the sun, but my face suddenly aged years in colors. Tell me. What exactly did you hear? Why are you talking "to me now, and what does it matter at this point? I don't understand," I added, raising my voice suddenly.

Only then did I notice that we had traveled the entire route. I don't remember the moment I got on the bus or that I was approaching my stop. "Alice, please wait," he said, and I bolted out of the bus like an arrow. The saddest part was that he didn't even try to run after me. I don't know why I wanted him to, but I thought that was exactly what he should have done.

The day started off strangely. My son fell ill, and unfortunately, I had to stay home with him for the entire week. Olaf was coming home later and more drunk each day. It seemed he couldn't be bothered to waste any time or energy on aggressive arguments and nightly fights. That was fine by me. The later he returned, the calmer I felt. I know this is no way to live, but for now, I don't have any other plan. After a week off—if you can call days spent caring for my son a break—I returned to work. I missed polishing glass, ironing shirts, and distributing beautifully scented towels.

My boss, Mr. Moyer, didn't greet me with a smile as usual. He was never a pleasant man, but I felt he liked me. I understand his disappointed expression. An older man with lots of wrinkles and dark glasses perched on his nose, which probably cost a fortune because they never slip down. Despite everything, he seems like a nice guy.

I can't quite remember the day I started working here. Our hotel has always been here, but it only started to be listed among the best in our area after Mr. Moyer bought it. The changes our boss introduced were spot-on. Being French with a great imagination, everything he did hit the bullseye. The hotel entrance is beautifully adorned with colorful flowers of every kind. The shutters are white with blue pots that beautifully complement the white marble windowsills. The windows feature white curtains decorated with small flowers. I've often found myself staring at these translucent curtains, billowing from a warm breeze through an open window during breakfast.

Today feels different. I keep thinking about what Max told me. This man intrigued me with his words. He is the first person in many years to pay any attention to me in any way, aside from asking me for the time or directions by older people. Or maybe I think about him because he is simply the type of man I don't have at home?

"Alice, hello"! Max runs up to me literally a second before I board the bus. "Why didn't you let me explain, especially since that's what you want?" he said with a sad expression, exactly how I imagine a sad face would look.

"Hello. That's too much information all at once. I don't know why I didn't let you explain," I politely respond to his question. "Please, just give me five minutes, and I'll explain everything," he says confidently, as if he knew I'd even give him ten minutes. So, I'm listening, I adjust my ponytail and place my hands on my hips. "I overheard your conversation with your boss completely by accident. I sometimes stayed at this hotel when..." his expression suddenly changed drastically. He turned pale, and I saw immense sadness in his eyes. "When my wife died. I couldn't stand being at home, looking at her pictures and drinking coffee from her cups, or sleeping in the same bed."
He suddenly ran his fingers through his hair and placed a hand on his cheek, as if ashamed to have said it aloud.

"I'm very, very sorry", I didn't know why, but I completely forgot about what he was supposed to explain. Instinctively, I hugged him right in the middle of the sidewalk. I genuinely felt just as sorry. "Alice, it's okay. I've long come to terms with it. It bothers me that I had to tell you this way, "he added and slightly pulled away from me. "I'm an oddball, but hearing your conversation and seeing you in the hotel really was a coincidence," he added.

"I'm sorry I was so harsh. I understand and see it's hard for you to talk about this" he said, and I felt like crying. It was as if another person had discovered my great secret. "You don't have to say anything. I understand your embarrassment," he concluded. Only then did I realize that my bus had left. To make matters worse, I stood for a good 10 minutes hugging some guy. Sure, he was sad, and so was I, but was that a reason to be hugging Max in front of other people? What if someone I know saw us? What if someone went to Olaf and told him what I was up to outside the home? To me, it was a hug meant to lift someone's spirits, but how does it look in the eyes of someone else? I have no idea.

"I think both our buses have left, "Max said, pulling me slightly away from him for a moment. The tone of his voice changed. From a sad tone, I felt a pleasant voice to my ears. """ he added. I shouldn't be going out for coffee with strange men. I live with a partner, if I can call him that." It's quite inappropriate, I said, quickly distancing myself from him. "But if it's just coffee, I'll take that on my shoulders," I added with a smile. His face also lit up as if I had said something that could suddenly change his entire world. I didn't know it then, but that was exactly what was about to happen.

We walked three, maybe five minutes to a café located next to the railway tracks. You might think that a place for coffee by the noise and loud sounds emitted by trains would be poor. And one might be mistaken. We entered the café via a small narrow path with disorderly laid stones. A large wooden sign reading coffee hung above the entrance, beautifully decorated with small, dried flowers. Underneath, wooden tables adorned with small, dried flowers hung under a canopy. Lots of lamps attached to a green jute rope hung from the ceilings. Around the seated people, green-silver fir trees of one size poked through. The noise of the approaching trains didn't bother at all.
I could even say it added more charm to the place. Something beautiful. I knew there was a café here, but I had never been. I don't leave the house often, especially not to cafés.

"What can I get you?" the waiter asked. "We have great latte. With every two coffees, we include a pumpkin bun," he added with a smile. "Alice, latte and a pumpkin bun" Max said, looking at me. His eyes were so familiar. I don't know why, but I felt very comfortable in his company. "I've never had such a bun," he added. "Sure! Latte and pumpkin buns," I said to the waiter.

"Tell me, what's really going on with you? I'm not used to dealing with strangers' issues, but I feel like you're not a stranger to me. Maybe it's nonsense, but I feel like I've known you for years," Max said. Strange because I thought exactly the same. "I want to get to know you better regardless. I feel like I can't let you just walk away. I feel like I'm somehow compelled to be near you. What am I saying, sorry. I don't want to scare you. But I feel the need to be honest. I don't have time, not to," he continued.

"I don't know what to say, Max. Now that I'm here with you, I feel similarly, but I know it's not appropriate. Besides, my feelings have never mattered much, and I think I've accepted that," I suddenly looked up at him. "You can't say that. Feelings are the most important. Why would you say that? It's nonsense," he threw back at me. "For years I've lived in a toxic relationship. I shouldn't even call it a relationship. My partner is very nervous and drinks a lot. Together with my son, we no longer feel safe in our own home."
I'd lived in this mire so long that I stopped seeing the world through rose-colored glasses, and I wondered what I was trying to achieve by saying such things to him.

"I suspected you had such problems. I saw your neck, I heard your boss. I see your somber expression. Why do you allow this? You're an interesting and attractive woman. You need to rise above this," Max said.

"I'm sorry you had to spend so much time worrying about a stranger from the hotel where you stayed. You didn't have to. I've lived this life for a long time. I manage," I replied. "Please, here's your coffee and buns. Enjoy!" the waiter interrupted us.

I should have been home long ago, picked up my son and returned. Time was flying relentlessly, yet I felt great in Max's company. For the first time in a while, someone noticed me, talked to me.
The freedom I felt during our meeting was very captivating. I started to see him in a different light. What first appeared as a curious stranger now seemed like a wonderful man. He is a

warm, kind person, and it feels like we could sit here every day, never running out of things to talk about.

After discussing the heavy topic of my personal life, we shifted to a completely different conversation. He told me about visiting his family in Greece, how he got lost and spent a night at a bus station. He talked about his interest in crime novels and documentaries. Of course, I shared similar things about myself. It had been a long time since I'd considered what I liked to do, what music I listened to, or which book I might pick up in a library. I had no one to talk about these things with. My life had stalled in a tiny apartment with a toxic person. Thankfully, I have my little angel, for whom I wake up every morning. If not for Adam, I wouldn't be here. Thanks to him, I know that someday I will get back on my feet and put everything back together. I have someone to do it for, but at the moment, I have no idea how.

It was time for our farewell. I think if it weren't for the fact that our coffee had long since finished and the weather had turned from sunny to gloomy, we might have sat there much longer. However, it was time for me. "Thank you for the coffee and for the pleasant time," I said to Max.

"This doesn't have to be our last meeting, Alice," he added. But it must be. Do you know what waits for me at home? "I can't afford to spend time like this. I have a son, I have a partner and..." I choked up. Max took my hand and gently pulled it towards him. "Alice, let someone help you. You don't have to go back there. I know that's not the place for you," he said with a saddened voice. "I can't let you leave today without a promise that we'll see each other again, and it won't just be at this bus stop," he added.
"I don't know what intentions you have towards me, but I don't want to drag you into my problems. I wouldn't forgive myself if I pulled more people down with me," I replied. "

What are my intentions? I thought they were clear. I looked for you, waited to run into you somewhere. What drew me to you couldn't have been a mistake." He lowered his head and placed it on my hand. "Please, let us get to know each other better... please let me... take care of you," he suddenly looked up again— "both of you," he added.

I always know what to say, even when my response is somewhat inappropriate. But this was the second time I was at a loss for words. We've only known each other for a few days, and it was our first time alone. Is it because of my low self-esteem? No. The answer is simple. It's fear of what will happen when Olaf finds out. I'm not one to hurt others. I'm not one to cheat, make loud exits from the home, slamming doors. That's not me. I have to do it the right way. Leave this man who is destroying my life, devouring me from the inside.

"Max, I don't know how to respond to what you're saying. We hardly know each other, and you're making promises like a teenager. Let's be adults. I have a terrible life, but I still share it with someone. I have nowhere to go, no place to hide. And even if... he'll find me and bring me back. It was very nice meeting you, but now I must go," I hoped my response seemed convincing, even though I didn't want to convince him.
"Please, give me your number. I'll call, we can talk. If something happens, you can count on me; I don't have anything so important that I couldn't help you," he looked at me with a kind and caring gaze, and I felt sorry for him.

"Sure. But don't call me after six, please," I replied and gave him my number. "It's a bad time to talk." Max wrote down my phone number on a white napkin and tucked the paper into the pocket of his gray jacket. "Take care, be safe," Max added.
"Of course. Goodbye." In a blink, I was already at the bus stop. I didn't look back once.

I was furious about the situation I was in. It's unfair when something nice happens for the first time in so long, and I can't grab that happiness for myself.

Chapter 5

The Night I Left

I couldn't sleep all night. I pondered everything that had been and what is now. I don't want to live like this. I decided to call Matilda. We've been friends for a long time, since high school. Even though we don't talk much, as she has her life and I have mine, when something serious happens, she tries to help me. I asked her if I could stay with her; "I want to leave Olaf, and I will do it today."

It would be about the twelfth attempt to leave behind those terrible times and years. Of course, she agreed. She told me to take care and call her if anything bad happened. We both knew what she meant.

Around five in the afternoon, I heard my phone ring. It's rare for anyone to call me. I rushed to the phone and immediately answered without checking who was calling. "Alice, how are you? Is everything okay? Did you get home safely?" a familiar voice spoke; it was Max.

"Hi, I see you're not ready for even a day of separation!," I said in a way that made me close my eyes in surprise. Could such a start to the conversation already be considered flirting? "Yes, I got home," I added. "I'm glad. How are you feeling?," Max continued. "I feel embarrassed but full of energy. Today, I plan to leave Olaf. You were right; I've been wondering what I'm actually doing here for a long time," I responded.

"What do you mean? Do you have a plan? Can I help you in any way?" He seemed very concerned, but for me, it was nothing new. I had packed my bags and tried to escape many times before, but I never succeeded.

"Don't think it's because of you. I've been trying to leave for several years. However, I never had enough courage to ask anyone for help. Today, I called a friend where we can stay until I figure out what to do next," I answered. I'm glad and worried. "Remember, if anything happens, you can call me" were the last words I heard. I quickly tucked the phone into my pants pocket.

Just then, Olaf came back. Why did he have to come back early today? I managed to pack everything and prepare, but I would have preferred more time. My suitcase was ready, and I had hung a backpack on the bathroom doorknob, close to the front door, so I could grab it quickly in case of more serious problems. In the backpack, I packed the most important things, from documents to work papers, health books for my son and me, and money I had secretly saved. I hoped I hadn't forgotten anything.

"I'm back!" I heard a shout from the living room. Olaf moved there strangely fast. Something was off. "We need to talk, I responded to his greeting." I didn't want to delay it. "What now?," he immediately took on a confrontational tone. "Olaf, we both know that things aren't working out. I need to leave you. And I'm going to do it today, right now," I began to shake, my face draining of blood. "What?" Olaf asked. "I'm leaving. I don't want to be with you anymore. I don't love you anymore. I don't know if I ever loved you. You've ruined my life. You're the last person who… "

Of course, he didn't let me finish. He hit me again, as a "true gentleman" would. This time he didn't bother to think it over and hit me lower or at least not with a fist. He treated me like a punching bag. Suddenly, I was locked in my room. For a good twenty minutes, I listened to insults and pleas for me to open those damn doors. And, in return, I yelled at him to shut up because he would wake up Adam.

Suddenly, I felt vibrations from my phone. I read a message from an unsaved number: Hang on a little longer, the police are on their way. I didn't have to wonder who the message was from; it was Max. However, something else puzzled me. How did he know what was happening? How did he know where to direct the police? And why did he do it?

Soon after, I heard the sound of a police car approaching, the creaking of the floor in our living room, and the flash of lights on our windows, followed by sharp, loud knocking on our door. "Mr. Olaf Jakus? Police. Please open the door," I heard one of the officers say. "Yes, how can I help?" Olaf responded, not opening the door. "We received a report of domestic violence. Please open the door. Your partner and son will be removed from your apartment immediately," the officer continued. Hearing this, my mouth dropped open so wide I felt my skin stretch uncomfortably. "I won't open the door for you," Olaf persisted. Then I heard a loud bang. The police had just broken down our door.

Everything happened so fast after that I'm not sure if I forgot to breathe. Two officers restrained Olaf, holding him away from the bedroom door where I had earlier locked myself in. They had to quiet him down as he screamed like a madman. Suddenly, his vocabulary seemed much more extensive. After a moment, one of the three officers knocked on my door. "Ms. Alice? Please come out. We are taking you away from here," he said in a kind but firm voice. "You won't be harmed, please open the door." I quickly went to Adam, who was sleeping, wrapped in a blanket on our bed, fortunately undisturbed by the entire unpleasant encounter. Heading to the door, I slung the previously packed backpack over my shoulder and grabbed the rolling suitcase in the other hand. Soon, one of the officers helped me. It only took seconds, and I was inside the police car. "It's okay now. You're safe.

"Where can we take you? I understand you have a place to stay," the officer spoke to me. "Yes. I'll give you the address," I said, my hands shaking so much that I couldn't enter Matilda's address into the navigation system. Thankfully, the officers were kind enough to do it for me.

After a moment, I realized we were about three kilometers away from that unfortunate apartment. That was enough for me; I felt that I could finally let go and be carried away by emotion. I cried for the entire twenty-five-minute drive to my friend's place.

Chapter 6

Max

My wife passed away at the age of thirty-two, and to make matters worse, it happened in spring, my favorite season. I met Victoria during high school. Fate had it that she fell in love with me at a college party I barely remember. That's where it all began. I always knew alcohol was bad for me.

I only remember how Victoria followed me around closely, never taking her eyes off me, which I found quite unpleasant. The party was a disaster. All my friends, including myself, were heavily intoxicated. About a month after that unsuccessful party, I received a call from my future wife. "Hi Max, are you there? Can you hear me well? I'm pregnant with your child," she said, laughing softly. This woman was absolutely not my type. I didn't want to go out to the movies with her or have drinks at a bar. She was a great friend to laugh with. That was it.

"What do you mean? But it was just that one time, Victoria. If you hadn't told me, I wouldn't have even remembered," I said, furious with myself. I was a calm guy who avoided such dramas. In a moment, I realized I had just ruined my life. Everything went smoothly afterward. Victoria became my wife, and the wedding was lavish only because it was organized by the bride's parents. It felt strange to stand at the altar, saying 'I do' without being sure about it. I suffered for a good six months.

This wasn't how I pictured marriage, family, and life together, especially not with someone you don't love. My wife was a beautiful woman, with long wavy hair, gorgeous large blue eyes, and a cute little nose. She was a walking queen, dressed in brand-name clothes and wearing only gold necklaces that perfectly sat on her protruding collar bones. I couldn't understand how I could not love her, but that was the case.

We spent a lot of time together, but I couldn't get myself to engage in this whole charade. She repeated, perhaps five times a day, how much she loved me and that she was the happiest person in the world. She was such an egotist that she never noticed I never said the same things back to her.

Two months later, I noticed messages on my wife's phone, "I will always love you and our little one. Pawel." Everything became clear then. The child she was carrying wasn't mine. Obviously, her partner with whom she had slept wasn't a suitable match for a wedding. I never wished anyone harm, but fate decreed that a few days after our argument about getting a divorce, Victoria lost the child and fell into depression. But I couldn't leave her alone. Despite how she had deceived me, she was still my wife. Whether I loved her or not, she was also a human being. I couldn't leave.

Victoria became withdrawn, but even so, she managed to apologize for what she had done. I knew she was madly in love with me, and I could never understand why. Shortly after one of our long discussions about our divorce, Victoria fell ill. It was malignant uterine cancer. Day by day, she became weaker, and for me, the days grew longer. She felt terrible all the time. Now, I couldn't leave her alone either; I would never forgive myself for that. My wife was always confident and insistent on having her way. But as the cancer took away her breath, I saw all that confidence burst like a soap bubble. Suddenly, she became a quiet, courage-less woman, walking from window to window all day, with breaks only for vomiting and sleep. She hardly ate and wanted nothing.

Despite what she had done to me, it pained me to see her fading away day by day. Victoria passed away a year after our wedding. I became a widower at such a young age. But it didn't matter. Maybe I will burn in hell for feeling this, but I felt relief in my heart. Not only was I finally free, but she was too, no longer having to suffer. I was with her until her last day.

After several years of solitude, travels to warm countries, and reading a few interesting books, I found myself back at this hotel. Since the house I lived in with Victoria was mine, I had to stay there and face the remnants of her presence. I didn't miss her, but it saddened me that my wife was gone. It didn't matter what kind of wife she was. I was furious that I had been deceived, yet proud that I managed to cope with it all.

Walking down the corridor to my room, I noticed a door slightly ajar, with big golden letters that read Director Moyer. Instinctively, I wanted to close the door, not understanding why I would do that. I slowed down before entering and suddenly overheard a conversation involving an older man and possibly his employee. Mr. Moyer was talking about the family situation of Alice and how she had been beaten again. I couldn't believe what I was hearing. I was shocked that in these times, there are still men who treat their women like that.

I quickly headed to my room, the conversation troubling me all evening. I picked up the hotel phone and requested two clean towels for the next morning, hoping that the unfortunate employee would bring them so I might be able to help her. My best friend is a policeman who deals with such cases, and he immediately came to mind.

The next morning, I was awakened by knocking. The towels are usually left in a decorative basket outside the door — curse me for not realizing that sooner. So, I headed to the restaurant downstairs. That's where I met her. I had never seen such beautiful, smooth skin as Alice's. Her cheeks were slightly blushed, and her long lashes held just a hint of mascara. Her beautiful dark shiny hair fell over her pale pink company shirt that bore the name Alice, which suited her perfectly. She was a gorgeous, delicate woman but had a hint of mischief. Never had I heard such a pleasant voice or seen such relaxed body movements. Her figure was like that of a youthful TV star — slim but not skinny, and definitely shorter than me. Everything about her was perfect.

I wondered what I was thinking to have such thoughts about a stranger. I had never been so captivated before. She was stunning; I felt I could go through hell with her. I watched Alice for a good half hour, noticing the polished glass at the restaurant bar. I was so mesmerized by her that I forgot why I was there. I thought about everything and nothing at the same time, sitting at an empty table for a good hour.

I wondered how anyone could hurt such a delicate and subtle woman. How could anyone raise a hand to anyone, let alone someone like her? I returned to my room but couldn't forget about her or her conversation with her employer. I decided to take matters into my own hands. I got out of bed and headed to Mr. Moyer's office. "Good morning. Mr. Moyer?"" I asked the man sitting behind the desk in a bold voice. "What can I do for you?" he replied kindly. "My name is Max Frans. I wanted to ask about an employee of this place, about Alice," I said, wanting to handle the matter quickly without unnecessary chat. "I'm not from the police, but I think I might know how I could help her. I heard your conversation a few days ago," I explained.

"Ah yes, Ms. Alice is a very good employee but has many problems at home," he replied without hesitation. "I am almost certain that she is being assaulted by her partner. She comes to work in a terrible state. She is an excellent worker, well-educated woman, and wonderful mother," finished the hotel manager.

"Could I possibly get her address? Maybe my friend could check out the situation," I asked politely. "Of course, I'll write it down for you right now," the man said, handing me the address written on a small yellow sticky note. I returned to my room with the note in hand. What should I do next? Maybe I shouldn't have gotten involved at all. I felt like I was trying to make up for lost years. I stood in the middle of the room, staring at the address. But what next?

Unable to just sit and do nothing, I decided to go to the bus stop from which Alice probably returned home. For several days in a row, I hadn't seen her, or maybe I hadn't recognized her? Finally, I saw her subtle, feminine walk. She had her hood pulled up, seeming to want to hide something. I decided to strike up a conversation, trying another day to explain how I knew her and that she shouldn't be afraid of me.

But it was all in vain. I felt I had frightened her, which was not my intention. Several times I was near her house, watching the shadows in the window, wondering if she was alright or if she would return in an even worse state the next day. Why was I so interested in this? It shouldn't have been my concern. When I finally exchanged a few words with her and persuaded her to have coffee at a beautiful cafe, I was overjoyed. I had never met a woman so intriguing and enchanting as her.

Many times I wondered how one could talk so interestingly about some movie or book. Her stories captivated me from head to toe. Each story started with a gentle smile on her face, as if she were flirting with me. When she spoke about something important to her, she did so with such passion that I forgot everything around us. I was impressed by how much one could say about home decor, a wedding outfit, or designing a child's room.

There was no topic we were lost in. She was wonderful, and I thanked fate for meeting her. I could sit with her in that cafe and just listen to her speak. No matter what she talked about, how she did it, or how long it took, nothing mattered to me when I was with her. When she left the cafe, I felt as if I had lost something.

I couldn't believe she had actually given me her phone number. I wouldn't be surprised if she had made it up just to get rid of me. I decided to send her a message, to call her. I wanted her to know she could count on me.

We had met only once, but I had already lost my head over her. I wasn't happy that I had made such big promises at our first meeting. But I was sure I didn't make them on a whim. What I feel for Alice happens once in a lifetime, and it had just happened to me.

After a wonderful evening at the cafe, I went to see my sister. We could always talk things through. Jowita was five years my senior. She had married a great guy and had two children. Ever since our parents divorced, and shortly thereafter our father passed away, I felt our relationship had grown stronger. I was glad to have such a wonderful sister.

"Max, what are you saying? You followed some poor girl? Have you completely lost your mind? You've always been a bit crazy, but this time, you've really lost it. I think you should see a psychiatrist," my sister responded to my ramblings about Alice. "Listen, you know me, and you know I don't do stupid things like that. I accept the life I have, but I've had enough. I want to help her. I want to be there for her, to be at her every call, to be whoever she needs me to be—why is that so hard to understand?," I hiss quietly at my sister.

"I understand. But isn't this too fast? She hasn't even left her partner yet. This is breaking up a family!" Hearing my sister's words, I glance at my watch. "It's time. We'll talk later, darling. Kiss the kids for me," I say, getting up and leaving the room. I don't even know if Jowita says anything else. I return home, grab my phone, and settle into my favorite blue armchair. Without thinking too much, I call Alice.

The moment I hear her wonderful voice, everything around me could disappear. We talk for a while, until suddenly, I stop hearing what she's saying. A lump forms in my throat, and I have no idea what to do next. A few moments later, I hear strange sounds—blows, then muffled cries from Alice. I know something is wrong. I have to act. For several minutes, I listen to the horrifying sounds of an attack on this young woman. My heart is racing. What else could I do? Go there myself? I might only make things worse. I wanted to be a hero, but not like this.

"Max, hey! What's up? It's late, is everything okay?" my friend answers. "Hey, you told me I could always count on you, right?" I ask. "Of course, talk to me," he says. "I met a woman…" I hear a friendly and familiar whistle on the other end. "No, no, it's not like that. Listen, I was just on the phone with her. She lives with an awful guy and has a small son. I was practically a witness to him abusing her. Can you do something?" I explain. "Shit, man, of course! Give me the address, I'll grab a buddy, and we're heading over. Tell me more—who is this guy? Does she have anywhere to go?" he asks.

I sent you the address in a message…" I start to say, but he cuts me off. Don't tell me it's Olaf's girl? "Damn, man… " Suddenly, my friend's tone changes. He continues, "That guy is completely unhinged. She's called the police multiple times, but she never had anywhere to go. She preferred to stay there rather than run, and even if she ran, he'd find her. I'm telling you, he's a psycho."

"Listen, get her out of there. If she has nowhere to go… bring her here. Text me when she's safe. Thank you, I knew I could count on you," I say, full of gratitude. "Of course, buddy. Give me half an hour, and it'll be taken care of. I'll message you. Talk soon." Our conversation ends. I stare at my phone like a zombie. I don't know what to do with myself. Why is this affecting me so much?

I've always believed in love at first sight, but how could it feel this serious? When I think about her piercing gaze, her warm voice, I feel like I'm going crazy. And knowing she's a good person, while life keeps beating her down—it's unbearable. As I'm lost in thought, a message arrives: "Max, she's safe. I took them to her friend's place. We'll stay in touch."

At that moment, I feel a weight lifted from my heart. Before going to sleep, I send Alice a short message. I want her to know I'm here. I know this is all crazy. We barely know each other. But who said love has to follow a timeline? I want to get to know her more everyday. I want to be by her side every night, to protect her and make her feel safe. Most important, I don't expect anything in return.

Of course, I'd be the happiest man alive if she gave me a chance to show her who I am—what kind of man I am and how much I'm willing to do for someone I care about. But if she decides that all she wants is friendship, I'll accept that too. For now, there's nothing else in my mind but Alice. I can wait for her forever. I just want to see her again, to take in her scent, to watch the way she bites her lower lip so sweetly.

Chapter 7

Safe, For Now

How wonderful it is to live in a world where Olaf doesn't exist. Even if just for a moment. Today, I can't stop smiling. Adam is happily playing with Matilda, building structures out of wooden blocks. What a beautiful sight. It's been so long since I felt this kind of relief. I sip my coffee on the terrace of my friend's house, watching them in disbelief. By staying here, I've managed to bring joy to two people at once. Matilda needs little ones around her, and my son is overjoyed by the attention she gives him.

But Max's message still lingers in my mind—the one I haven't replied to. It's already been three days. What should I do? Text him back or call him already! "I can't stand watching you like this, sunshine!" Matilda, as always, gives me a much-needed push with just one sentence. At that moment, I pick up my phone and start typing: Hi Max. Thank you for your help, you really didn't have to do that. I don't know how you're doing, but we're all right. Stay in touch. Alice. I must have read that message at least 150 times before finally pressing send. The next two minutes feel like an eternity. Then I hear the sound of my phone vibrating. I unlock it instantly and read the reply: Hey. I'm so glad to hear you're okay. I was really worried. I'd love to see you and talk about a few things. Let me know when you're free, and I'll come to you. Max. P.S. Remember, I'm not a spy. Reading that message, I even smiled.

Living without Olaf felt strange. The evenings were quiet, peaceful. I could sit in an armchair, watch a show, and pour myself a glass of wine. I can't even remember the last time I spent my time like this. But I'm scared that this bubble will burst soon.

"So, did you answer him? Please, just tell me! Otherwise, I'm checking your phone myself," Matilda teases. "I haven't replied yet. I have no idea what to write," I answer. "What do you mean?

We're getting you all dolled up, and you're going on a date! If you don't come back tonight... don't worry, your son is the greatest joy that has ever happened to me!" Matilda says, trying to convince me.

I had a serious conversation with Matilda about how long I could stay at her place and under what conditions. She had only been living in her apartment for six months, and now she was able to help me. Before that, she lived with her grandmother, whom she took care of, and she simply didn't have the option to offer me shelter. She had been encouraging me to leave Olaf for a long time, but my fear kept me from going anywhere beyond work. Of course, she warned me that if I ever went back to him, she would never speak to me again. And I knew she meant it.

I waited half an hour before typing a message: I'm finally free. I assume you know where I am, so we can meet. Today? Tomorrow? Let me know what time and what I should wear. P.S. I think a spy would have better fashion sense. I didn't have to wait long. My phone vibrated three minutes later: Perfect! Tonight, 7 PM, at your friend's place. Bringing a few outfit options—I have no idea where we'll end up. P.S. Your sense of humor is a solid 10/10. Can't wait. – Max. A smile stayed on my face for at least fifteen minutes.

The clock showed 5:30 PM. I figured an hour and a half was plenty of time to get ready. Considering my daily routine, where getting myself together usually takes no more than seven minutes, I thought this would be easy. Of course, I was wrong. I was ready just in time, right before 7:00 PM. I took a long bath in Matilda's enormous tub, listening to Beyoncé. I figured her songs would set the perfect mood for the evening and keep me in high spirits.

I left my hair in a natural, slightly messy style, it's how I feel best. My dark, wavy locks cascaded down my back, looking much better than usual. Maybe it was thanks to Matilda's high-end hair products, which she swears by. For once, I applied more mascara than usual and shaped my eyebrows using a special brow shadow. To top it off, I painted my lips with a matte brownish-burgundy lipstick and added a touch of blush to my cheeks. I pulled out a navy-blue short dress from deep inside my suitcase—one meant for special occasions that never seemed to happen. It was charming, dusted with subtle glitter that wasn't visible from afar. My shoulders were bare, and the dress ended mid-thigh. Oh my God. How do I even look? That thought hit me immediately.

"You look stunning! Honey, look at your gorgeous mama!" Matilda shouts from the hallway. "Sweetheart, put on those black heels. And, most important, perfume! I don't know if you have any, but your favorite one is on my bathroom shelf. I know you love it, and I've been using a different one lately. It's yours now!" she says with a bright smile. "Do I even look like myself?" I ask, heading toward the bathroom to use the perfume. "I feel so strange," I add. "Honey, you look like you—when you're truly living," Matilda says.

We smile at each other, and I know she genuinely wants the best for me. I know she hopes this evening will let me forget my troubles, even if just for a while. And I know that spending the night with my son is pure happiness for her. "I'm off. Have fun!" I say to Matilda. "Oh, sweetheart, I definitely will! And I hope you have just as much fun," Matilda replies, then adds after a short pause, "If anything happens, call me. Be careful." With those words, she closes the door behind me.

I didn't have to wait long. After just two minutes, I spotted a Volvo pulling into the parking lot. I was surprised that I had arrived before him. Slowly, I walked past the other mud-splattered cars, glanced through the passenger window, and knocked lightly. Max rolled down the window, giving me a small smile. A moment later, I saw him engage the handbrake without turning off the engine and step out of the car.

"Good evening, Alice. I hope you didn't have to wait for me," he said as he walked toward me. "I just stepped out a minute ago. No waiting needed. How are you?" I asked. Max stopped about a meter away from me, his eyes gleaming. "How am I? If you're doing well, then I am too. Please, get in, he said," moving toward the passenger door and opening it for me in one swift motion. "Have a seat."

As I stepped into the car, a pleasantly sweet scent of vanilla filled my senses. I had no idea how he knew — or if he even did — but vanilla was my favorite scent. A perfect guess. One point in his favor. I noticed a bottle of mineral water in the door compartment and a phone charger plugged in. What I didn't see was the usual mess that I had encountered in so many other cars I had been in before.

"Where are we going?" I asked with a smile. "I don't know if you like surprises, so I'll tell you everything I have planned," he said, flashing a bright smile that showed his straight white teeth. "We'll start with dinner at a restaurant, then take a walk, which will lead us to a concert." "Whose concert? And how do you even know I like concerts?" I asked, raising an eyebrow. "We're going to see a few different artists. I don't know all of them, and I'm not sure if it'll be worth it, but I was curious about what kind of music people are into these days. From what I read, it's supposed to be fun and danceable. And honestly, I have no idea if you like concerts — but I do," Max explained.

Within minutes, I had completely forgotten about all my problems. A restaurant, a walk, and a concert, what a perfect evening. Spending time together, talking, and having fun all at once. A great plan. The restaurant Max chose turned out to be my ultimate culinary dream come true. Somehow, he had picked sushi. I adore sushi of all kinds. The moment we sat down at the table, I felt completely at ease with Max. Once again, we never ran out of things to talk about.

Our table was set in the restaurant's garden, surrounded by a small stream filled with floating lilies and delicate lights that blended beautifully with the colors of the flowers. The water reflected the moonlight, and in the background, soft, romantic music played. A perfect place, I thought.

But it wasn't the location that made the biggest impression on me. Max looked like a movie star. I could have sworn he had taken longer to get ready than I had. He wore a perfectly pressed white shirt with silver buttons. The buckle of his belt nearly blinded me with its shine. On his wrist, he wore a black sports watch. And that was all I remembered about his outfit—because I had spent most of my time admiring his face. There wasn't a single flaw. His skin was just as flawless as the first time I saw him. His slightly crooked nose caught a few stray locks of his tousled blond hair. I never thought I'd look at a man like this. Not just any man. But at him? I could.

When I saw her standing by my car, I couldn't believe it was really her. She looked like an angel. I couldn't take my eyes off her. I felt like I had to keep looking, to memorize every detail of her. She smelled sweet, a mix of honey and lemon. Her cheeks were slightly flushed, and her beautiful, wavy, glossy hair cascaded over her shoulders. I had never met a woman as breathtakingly beautiful as her.

The thought of everything she had been through made me clench my fists. Thankfully, she didn't notice. I opened the door for her, and she slowly slid into the passenger seat. I never thought I'd have to fight so hard to control myself around a woman. If I followed my instincts, I would have pulled the handbrake, taken her hand, and told her I'd take her to the ends of the earth. I could have cupped her delicate face in my hands and kissed her endlessly. So many thoughts and desires swirled in my mind, but I had to hold myself back.

The sushi idea came to me completely by chance. Taking a woman on a first date to a pizzeria felt like a weak move. I had chosen our table and even the music playing near us when I made the reservation. The restaurant had a warm and cozy atmosphere. The air smelled of incense, and each table was adorned with soft, glowing candles. Chinese lanterns hung from the ceiling, casting just enough light onto our table. This was exactly the ambiance I had hoped for. We ordered sushi and a carafe of red wine.

My plan was to leave my car in the restaurant's parking lot and pick it up tomorrow. I wanted to enjoy this evening with a glass of champagne or wine—after all, it was a perfect complement to any date. I wasn't planning to rush home. The concert wouldn't start until after eleven, so there was no way I'd catch a bus back. I was already counting on taking a taxi home. I couldn't take my eyes off Alice. I had to remind myself not to sit there staring at her with my mouth open as she spoke.

In the lantern's glow, she looked even more stunning. Her dress sparkled more than it had in my car. I noticed tiny shimmering specks that reflected on her chin and décolletage. Her curves were perfect—her full, round breasts, her slightly protruding tummy that only added to her charm. She was slender yet beautifully shaped, her body radiating femininity.

I am a gentleman. I don't look at women in an inappropriate way—I respect her. But tonight, I had to seriously restrain myself. I often glance at women passing by on the street, but I never had a particular type. I had always believed the right one would find her way to me. But no woman had ever held my gaze for this long. I had the feeling that she would hold it forever. We talked about places we wanted to visit one day, about famous actors, and about exotic spices—I never knew some of them could be so expensive. We discussed overpriced apartments in the area and the ridiculously cheap bus tickets in other parts of the city.

I had never spoken so freely and effortlessly with anyone before. We spent long moments laughing and joking lightheartedly. She sat in front of me, smiling, free. Tonight was a perfect choice. And I felt like I had known her forever. I glanced at my watch—it was just after ten. I had completely lost track of time. We should be heading toward the square where the concert was about to start. I had always loved concerts, but I never really had anyone to go with. My friends preferred going to bars and drinking. My ex-wife was never the type for events like these. She might have accidentally stained her new shoes or gotten splashed with beer from someone's cup. That would have been unthinkable.

I signaled for the waiter and asked for the bill. "Shall we get going, darling?" As I said it, I suddenly realized how I had addressed her. It felt strangely natural to call her that, but I was nervous about her reaction. Still, I didn't correct myself. "Of course, it's time. We don't want to be late," Alice responded, completely unfazed by my slip-up. Perfect. "If the beginning of the evening was already this amazing, I can't wait for the rest!"

I sent her a warm, affectionate smile as I stood up and walked over to pull out her chair. "Oh, thank you!" she said, appreciating the gesture. As we stepped out of the restaurant, I instinctively wanted to take Alice's hand, but I stopped myself at the last second. We weren't high schoolers holding hands, nor were we kids asking each other, Will you be my girlfriend? Besides, it was way too soon. Alice had too much on her mind to think about another relationship right now, and I completely understood that.

That's why I made it my goal to erase gray memories from her past and show her that from this moment on, she had someone she could rely on. I would always try to protect her and her son. Still, that didn't change the fact that I would have loved to walk to the concert with our fingers intertwined. But once again, I held myself back.

"You know, I forgot to ask you something. What do you do for a living? I feel like I already know so much about you, yet I completely overlooked such a simple question. Aside from playing silent detective, do you do anything else?" Alice smiled and glanced at me. "I'm listening."

Aside from my detective work on the side," I chuckled, "I'm actually an architect. I really enjoy my job, but it takes a lot of training and experience to become a good one. I design houses—that's my daily work. Most of the time, I work from home; it's quieter there, and I can focus better," I explained, slipping my hands into my pockets. I figured it was safer that way.

"Oh wow, that's amazing! It's great that you enjoy what you do. Not everyone is that lucky," she said, raising an eyebrow in admiration. "And you? What would you be doing if you didn't have to work at the hotel? Not that I'm judging where people work, but I doubt that's your dream job. You're capable of so much more. Then again, if it weren't for the hotel, I never would have met you," I said as I gently guided her to the other side of the sidewalk. I had just realized she had been walking closest to the street—the dangerous side. Her place was on the inside, where it was safer.

Without noticing my small gesture, Alice answered, "I'm a florist by profession. I love arranging flowers into beautiful bouquets. But I couldn't find anything interesting nearby, and I needed a job immediately, so I ended up at the hotel. Like you said, it's not my dream job. My real dream is to own a little flower shop on the corner. I'd welcome people with a smile, hang a tiny bell on the door, and arrange colorful cards for every occasion on the counter. That would be perfect."

Now I knew where she wanted to be, what she wanted to do, and what made her happy. We hadn't talked much about our love lives, but we already knew the most important things. I was an unhappy widower, deceived by the woman I once trusted. She was a single mother, broken by the man who was supposed to love her. Different struggles, yet so similar.

As we walked to the concert, I asked her about her son, and her eyes instantly lit up. A warm smile spread across her face. She spoke about her child with such love that I had never witnessed before. She was the most devoted mother on earth, willing to do absolutely anything for him—and, I suspected, for many other people as well. I loved listening to her talk about how Adam took his first steps, how he started eating with his little fingers from his own plate. Every story she shared brought a smile to my face as well. I had never seriously thought about my future with children. I never had a partner who would throw herself into the fire for our kids—or for me, for that matter. Unfortunately, that kind of love had never been part of my reality. But as I walked beside her, listening to these beautiful stories, I realized something—when you have a woman by your side who can play a thousand roles, who embraces life in all its forms, then you are the luckiest man alive. And I would do anything to stand by her side forever.

We arrived at the concert just in time. The venue was so brightly lit that it was impossible to miss. We could see the glowing lights from far away. I didn't know exactly what kind of music they would be playing, but it didn't really matter. The smile on Alice's face was enough. I knew that both of us needed a night like this. We had faced enough hardships in our lives—it was finally time to enjoy ourselves.

We made our way right up to the stage, where we could hear the upbeat sounds of pop music. Perfect. I didn't usually listen to this kind of music, but at that moment, the lively melody felt just right. We started moving gently to the rhythm, letting the music take over. Alice lifted her arms above her head, swaying freely, and I instinctively placed my hand on her hip. In some way, I wanted to show everyone around us that she was here with me. I didn't know why I felt the need to do that, but it seemed romantic in a subtle way. She didn't seem to mind, so I didn't move my hand away.

As we danced together, moving closer with each beat, she rested her hands on the back of my neck. The song shifted into a slower rhythm, no longer the kind you jump wildly to. The atmosphere softened. And then, before I even knew how it happened, her lips brushed against mine. I was surprised, but I didn't hesitate to return the kiss. It was a moment I hadn't planned at all—but one I never wanted to end.

How did this happen? After such a wonderful evening at the restaurant, I couldn't control myself. From the moment I got into his car, I felt strange flutters in my stomach. And when he pulled out my chair at the table, I caught the sweet scent of his cologne—it made my head spin.

I had no idea if he would pull away or tell me it was too soon. But to my surprise, he returned my gentle kiss. Our lips met in a way no one had ever kissed me before—so softly, as if it were both our first and last kiss. Max pulled me closer, and I instinctively dug my nails into the back of his neck. It was incredible. We stood there for what felt like forever. Then, he slowly pulled back, his hands still wrapped around my waist. He cupped my cheek with one hand and brushed his nose against mine. It was one of the sweetest moments I had ever experienced.

I was surprised by how such small gestures could bring so much happiness. And before I could process what was happening, I felt his lips on mine again. This time, the kiss was deeper, more intense. His hands wandered a little lower than before. "Would you like something to drink?" Max asked as he pulled away slightly, his voice warm. "Definitely! My throat is so dry," I replied with a smile. He grinned back. "Want to come with me?"

"Don't worry, I'll wait here. I'm not going anywhere," I assured him. With that, Max disappeared into the crowd. I stood there for about ten minutes, swaying to the music. In the distance, I saw the long line stretching from the wooden bar near the stage. Then, out of nowhere, I felt someone tap me roughly on the shoulder. "What are you doing here? Does Olaf know what you're up to?" a male voice sneered. I turned and immediately recognized my ex-partner's best friend. He reeked of alcohol, looking like he'd been drinking since noon. "Leave me alone," I said firmly. "Leave you alone?" he scoffed. I'm taking you back where you belong. You took the kid too, didn't you? You'll regret this.

I didn't even have time to react before he grabbed my arm and started pulling me toward the exit. I felt completely powerless. I wasn't strong enough to fight back, and the music was too loud for anyone to hear me. Then, suddenly, I felt myself being pulled back in the opposite direction—but gently, with a touch that reminded me of Max. "If you touch her again, you'll regret it,"

Max's voice was sharp, controlled, but furious. I had never seen him like this before. His face darkened, his jaw clenched, and his hands curled into fists. He stood tall, his presence alone commanding respect. I was relieved that he was there, but I had never been in a situation like this before—I could only stand frozen, waiting to see what would happen next.

"That's my buddy's girl, you idiot. I'm taking her home," the man slurred. Funny, I hadn't even bothered to remember his name. The moment he stepped toward me again, Max blocked his path. Unlike Olaf's friend, Max was well-built and taller, making me feel safe beside him. Without hesitation, Max raised his arm and punched the guy square in the face. "I'm not going to say it again," he growled as the man stumbled back, falling onto the ground. "We'll meet again," Olaf's friend muttered, clutching his face.

Max ignored him and took my hand, leading me toward the restroom area. As we walked through the crowd, people instinctively moved aside, as if they had all witnessed what had just happened. My heart was racing—I couldn't even catch my breath. "What just happened?" I whispered. "Are you okay? Does anything hurt? That guy was a complete disgrace," Max said, stopping beside the restroom entrance. He leaned in closer, scanning me for any injuries. "I'm fine," I reassured him. "Can we just leave? Do you know a different place we could go?"

"I had no intention of spending the rest of our date here anyway," he said with a playful smirk. Then, slowly, he placed a soft kiss on my forehead before taking my hand and leading me away from the concert venue.

For the next few minutes, Max walked in silence, holding my hand so gently as if he were afraid he might hurt me. Every now and then, he glanced at me to make sure I was okay. I knew I should have felt unsettled by what had happened, maybe even afraid of what the future held if I continued trying to live my own life. But I didn't think that way anymore. For the first time, I didn't run away. For the first time, I didn't grab my things and return to my abuser, only to be greeted with a slap or forced intimacy I never wanted. For the first time, I had someone who stood up for me. And that meant everything.

"We can sit in the garden, relax on the lounge chairs, and listen to whatever music you like. I want to make sure this evening stays enjoyable for you," Max suggested. "On the way, we can stop by a great restaurant and grab something to go. I also have a pool—we could go for a swim. What do you think?"

For a moment, I hesitated. Was it really appropriate to go to his house on our first date? But instead of following that thought, I found myself responding in a way that completely contradicted it. "Sure! That sounds amazing!" I said enthusiastically.

On the way to Max's house, we stopped at a small Italian restaurant, famous for serving the best pasta in the area. I didn't spend too much time deciding what to order, it didn't really matter. We got two pasta dishes, and as a surprise, they threw in a complimentary bottle of Italian wine. They must have noticed we were on a date. Though for us, the real part of the evening was just beginning.

Max's house wasn't far from the concert venue. As we pulled into the driveway, I noticed the soft glow of small white lanterns lining the entrance, and a neatly trimmed hedge encircling the property. The house looked incredibly cozy, about 150 square meters, with a spacious garden. In the distance, I spotted a small pool surrounded by vibrant, colorful flowers. Every window stretched down to the ground, and only a few of them had delicate curtains that cascaded onto the floor.

Just like before, Max opened my door, then gently took my hand and guided me toward the entrance. Inside, his home felt just as warm and inviting as it looked from the outside. Framed photographs and paintings decorated the walls, while candles, incense sticks, and white lanterns were scattered throughout the space. A wide hallway led to a large, open concept living room and kitchen, and to the left, we passed by a bathroom and a bedroom. The kitchen was softly illuminated by the moonlight reflecting off the pool water outside.

The entire house was designed in soft beige and warm brown tones. It was simple, yet so uniquely put together. I was genuinely surprised that a man could have such an eye for color coordination and interior details. It was absolutely my style—I felt instantly comfortable within these walls.

As we stepped into the living room, my eyes were immediately drawn to the grand white fireplace. Opposite it, two brown armchairs with golden stitching were perfectly arranged, adding an elegant yet cozy touch. The dim lighting created an effortlessly romantic atmosphere. I had a feeling Max hadn't set this up just for tonight. This ambiance seemed to match his personality. I could easily picture him sitting here, lost in thought with a book in hand, or reflecting on deep, intriguing topics.

Between one of the armchairs and the fireplace stood a small wooden table, stacked with an old radio and a vintage record player. On the floor, scattered in a seemingly chaotic yet artistic manner, were vinyl records by different artists. I couldn't take my eyes off this fascinating little corner—it was effortlessly cool.

As I glanced at my phone, a new message from Matilda popped up: Just so you know, everything is perfect here! I just wrapped your son in a tight cuddle, and we don't miss you at all! If you come back late—DO NOT wake us up under any circumstances! Your Matilda. PS: Don't forget protection! Love. A smile spread across my face as I tucked my phone back into my bag. With a deep breath and a confident step, I walked further into the room, ready for whatever the rest of the night had in store.

Chapter 8

Learning to Breathe

I designed my home with taste, but without excessive effort. I picked everything myself, wanting this space to reflect who I was. I wanted to feel at ease, free of pressure, yet still surrounded by elegance. What I hadn't expected was how much this place would intrigue Alice. I couldn't help but smile when she stood in the living room, mouth slightly open, eyes shining as she admired the fireplace. I wasn't in the habit of bringing women home—certainly not on a first date. In fact, I couldn't recall doing so on a second or third date either. But this was different. Being with Alice felt natural, effortless. I wanted her to feel that too. I hadn't planned on bringing her here tonight; the thought hadn't even crossed my mind earlier. But after what happened, I had no choice. I didn't want to take her to a bar—not after what she had just been through. This was the safest place she could be. And where would she feel more secure than here, in my home, with me?

From the moment she stepped inside, Alice curiously wandered through my living room, glancing at photographs and flipping through records stacked near the fireplace. A comfortable silence filled the space until I decided to break it. "Something to drink? Coffee? Tea? Wine? Are you hungry? Maybe some pasta? Or a movie?" I fired off a series of questions. "Wait, wait! Let me think for a second before I answer all that," she laughed. "Take your time, we've got all night," I grinned.

"I'd love a glass of that Italian wine. It's too late for coffee, and I don't drink tea often—tea is for dark winter evenings with a book, my dear. I'm not hungry, maybe we can order something later. Just don't make me choose—I'm terrible at deciding what to eat!" she said, giggling. "Got it! Wine coming right up," I said, turning toward the kitchen. I grabbed two glasses from the cabinet and set them on the kitchen island, then pulled the bottle of semi-sweet rosé from the bag.

As I poured the wine, I glanced up and saw Alice settling into one of my armchairs. She crossed her feet beside the golden legs of the chair and slowly kicked off her heels while holding one of my vinyl records in her hands. It was one of the most beautiful sights I had ever witnessed. She looked like a vision, like a lady from an old movie. No one would have guessed that just yesterday, she was walking through the halls of a hotel with a weary expression, carrying stacks of towels.

Alice didn't have to try, she was effortlessly stunning, like a queen without a throne. My chest tightened at the thought of everything she had been through. She deserved better—so much better. And if I had even the slightest chance of giving her that, I'd do whatever it took. With two glasses of wine in hand, I walked toward her. She looked up, smiling warmly before glancing back at the Bon Jovi record, she was studying. I took the seat beside her and handed her a glass.

"I see you listen to just about everything. That's great—I think it's boring to limit yourself to one artist or one genre, she said enthusiastically. And just like that, another conversation unfolded, leading to another, and another. We could have talked all night. We started with music, then moved on to movies, and somehow, we even ended up discussing royal family gossip and Hollywood scandals. We laughed, drank, and barely noticed when the first bottle of wine disappeared.

We talked about photography techniques, different types of wall paints, and everything in between. I watched her closely, memorizing every detail. I studied her every movement, learning the subtle variations of her smiles. One was the most genuine I had ever seen when she talked about her son. Another was mischievous, like when I accidentally spilled a drop of wine on her hand while refilling her glass. Then there was one that was soft, romantic, accompanied by a slight blush on her cheeks.

Everything about her fascinated me. Sometimes, I forgot what I was saying because I was too focused on her lips—soft and pink, perfectly shaped. Strands of her dark hair occasionally fell across her face, and she absentmindedly tucked them behind her ear. Once, she was so lost in conversation that a lock of hair fell straight into her wine glass, and she didn't even notice. It was adorable. I glanced at my watch. 2:15 a.m. I couldn't believe we had been sitting there for so long.

"Maybe we should go for a swim? That is, of course, if the master of the house allows it," Alice teased. "You want to swim in my pool at two in the morning?" I replied with a playful question.
"I understand if you don't want to. It was a silly idea, sorry. Sometimes I forget myself and feel too comfortable," she added. "Don't apologize! Are you jumping in as you are, or do you need a moment?" I asked with a grin.

With a swift movement, Alice set her wine glass down on the wooden table and leaned toward me, grabbing my hand while flashing one of her warm, romantic smiles. Without hesitation, I followed her. She led me quickly toward the garden doors, and within moments, we stood by the steps leading into the pool, right beside the lounge chairs. As usual, I managed to bump my shin against one of the metal frames, but at that moment, I barely felt the pain.

The moon cast a silver glow over the water's surface, and the lanterns I had left on illuminated the area, giving it a soft, romantic ambiance. Alice moved closer and began unbuttoning my shirt. Her movements, once energetic, suddenly turned slow and deliberate. Her face took on an alluring expression, her smile playful and inviting.

Following her lead, I reached for the zipper of her elegant dress. She looked stunning in it, but I had a feeling that seeing her without it would take my breath away. Before I could fully process what was happening, my shirt slid to the ground, and in the next moment, her dress followed.

We stood there, looking at each other in silence, revealing more than just our bodies—our souls. Alice broke the silence first, grinning mischievously as she unfastened my belt before dashing toward the pool. Within seconds, she was fully submerged in the water. It was probably for the best—I had no idea how much longer I could have stood there, frozen in place, as she looked at me like that.

"Do you always take this long to make a move?" she teased, waving me over. Her dark hair floated gently on the water's surface, illuminated by the moonlight. She looked stunning, even more so than before. I had swum in this pool alone countless times at night, but tonight, it felt different. Everything had a purpose. I slipped into the water and swam toward her.

When I surfaced, I saw her resting her elbows on the edge of the pool, watching me closely. I wasn't sure what came over me. Before I realized it, Alice was in my arms, her hands tangled in my hair. Her legs wrapped gently around my waist, and I could feel her warmth close to me. I held her securely, one hand resting on her back, the other at her waist. Our kiss was deep, intense, and filled with emotions neither of us could put into words. It was like one of those moments in romantic films when two people finally reunite after being apart for too long.

I felt the weight of everything we had both been through and the quiet promise of something new, something real. I traced my hands gently down her back, holding her close, but as my fingers brushed over her thigh, I felt her suddenly tense. "What's wrong? Do you want me to stop? Just say the word," I asked softly. "No, it's nothing… Everything is wonderful. I just… I feel self-conscious," she admitted, lowering her gaze to the water. "What is it?" I pressed gently.

Alice hesitated before placing a hand on the inside of her thigh, as if trying to cover something. Carefully, I moved her hand aside and noticed a long scar running across her skin. It wasn't fresh, but it wasn't old either. Dread settled in my chest. I had a horrible suspicion of what might have happened. The scar stretched at least twenty centimeters. I looked at Alice's expression and saw the sadness in her eyes.

"What happened?" I asked, my voice was quiet but firm. "Olaf, "she whispered, and instantly, my fists clenched. Anger surged through my veins. "He did this to you. With what? When? Why? Tell me everything," I said as gently as I could, trying to keep my rage in check while examining the scar.

"About a year ago, I started resisting him… refusing to be with him like that. But to him, it was his right. It hurt, Max. It hurt so much. He would take what he wanted in the middle of the night, and when I finally fought back, he stabbed me. He said he'd scar me so no one else would ever want me," she explained, her voice breaking.

Hearing her words was like a knife to my own heart. Before she could say another word, I pulled her into a tight embrace and pressed a tender kiss on her forehead. "It's over now. To me, every inch of you is perfect—with or without scars. Today, tomorrow, always. You are beautiful. Be mine," I whispered. I saw a single tear roll down her cheek. I held her tightly, unwilling to let her go.

At that moment, I knew—I would do everything in my power to make sure she never had to feel that kind of pain again. Before I realized it, I was carrying her in my arms, out of the water, into the warmth of my home, where she would finally be safe.

This was, without a doubt, the best night of my life. From the moment I laid Alice down on my bed and we made love, I remember every single detail so vividly that I know I will never be able to forget it. In the past, sex with women had never lasted long. I never saw the point in romantic gestures, nor did I pay much attention to whether my partner was truly satisfied. I just did what I had to do, got up, and walked away. But this time, everything was different.

We made love over and over again, yet I still couldn't get enough. Our bodies, still damp from the pool water, now glistened with beads of sweat. We became one. I had been so wrong about intimacy. I had never looked at it this way before. With every passing minute, Alice became even more beautiful to me. Her scent, her breath—they drove me to the edge of madness.

Should I have asked myself if I was enough for her? If she was truly enjoying herself? I didn't need to wonder. I regretted that my bedroom wasn't soundproof because, from the way she reacted, I was certain—I had passed the test. Every time we finished, she would look deep into my eyes as if she were about to ask for more. But she didn't need to. I couldn't get enough of her.

She was the first woman I had ever brought into my bedroom, the first woman I had ever slept with on a first date. This was never the plan. I hadn't brought her here for this. But with every moment, I was losing my mind over her. And I was afraid—afraid that it would all end too soon. I refused to let the dark thoughts of the past few days take over. We made love under the soft glow of candlelight, the air filled with the scent of lavender incense—the first thing my hands had found in the shadows of my bedroom. I kissed every inch of her skin, over and over, and yet it was never enough.

As she lay beside me, before we gave in to each other again, I traced each beauty mark on her body, memorizing them as if they were constellations in my sky. I wanted to know everything I saw by heart, to rediscover her every time, like an unending journey. I became completely absorbed in learning what made her shiver, what made her sigh in bliss. I loved the way she would let out the softest breath whenever she brushed her lips against the edge of my ear. What happened between us was more than just passion—it was a love story. One I never wanted to end.

And for the first time, it wasn't just about me. It wasn't about my own satisfaction. More than anything, I cared about her. Alice was so tender, yet so incredibly passionate in everything she did that I forgot where I was. She touched me with confidence, with purpose, leaving me wanting for nothing. Every time we came together, I had to bite my lip, forcing myself to hold on just a little longer, just so I could feel her a little more.

This was not how the night was supposed to end. At least, that's what all my friends used to say. Don't be late for a date. Don't drink alcohol on a date. Don't order fish. And absolutely don't sleep with him on the first or even the second date. Clearly, I hadn't been a diligent listener. But honestly, I had no idea why anyone should dictate what I wanted or how I wanted it. The most beautiful date of my life. I had waited so long for something like this.

From the moment Max carried me from the pool to his bedroom, I couldn't catch my breath just thinking about it. Not to mention everything that had happened between us. The man I had only met a few days ago was now lying beside me, naked, pressing a kiss to my forehead. The way he had devoted himself to me last night had exceeded all my expectations. His hands had traveled so effortlessly over every inch of my body. His lips had fit perfectly into every curve and crevice of my skin. The moments from last night would never leave me.

When I opened my eyes, I met Max's gaze. I had a feeling he'd been awake for some time already. It felt strange to wake up beside someone. I wondered what he saw in me. And then, before he could say anything, the memories of last night flashed through my mind in an instant. How he grazed my nipples with his teeth, how his tongue moved in slowly pulsing motions over my most sensitive places. How he pulled me into his arms with such strength, while I surrendered to him completely, soft as a woolen doll.

I wasn't even sure how many times we had done it. I had never spent a night like that before. I never knew that someone could make intimacy feel so... limitless. That any man would make my pleasure his focus. My thoughts scattered when Max's voice broke the silence. "Good morning," he whispered before pressing another kiss to my forehead. "I can't take my eyes off you." He smiled, and this time, he kissed me deeply on the lips. "Good morning," I replied.

"I was waiting for you to wake up. I want to say right away that last night, I tried my best. I wanted to see you happy. But I also need you to know... bringing you here wasn't about taking you to my bed." His expression grew slightly more serious. "I wanted this," I interrupted him. "I started it. I wanted you." I leaned in and kissed the tip of his nose. Max ran his fingers gently along my cheek, then sat up beside me, leaning against the headboard. That's when I noticed—he had changed his position to keep me from seeing or feeling his arousal. But without a second thought, my hands found their way to him. As if, from now on, this was my duty, my right. "Alice...,"Max murmured. "Max...," I whispered, locking eyes with him. We didn't need to say anything else. We understood each other without words.

In one swift motion, Max pulled me onto his lap, holding me firmly by the waist. I barely had time to catch my breath before he was inside me again. His hands gripped my hips, guiding my movements in a slow, intoxicating rhythm. His tongue traced lazy circles along my neck and breasts. The way our bodies moved, the sounds that escaped my lips—none of it mattered anymore. Nothing else existed but us.

Chapter 9

The Shape of Trust

His bedroom was just as cozy as the rest of the house. But here, in this space, was the heart of it all. The bed was wooden and sturdy, covered in white sheets adorned with tiny blue flowers so faint that I barely noticed them.

I wasn't consciously trying to memorize the details of every room, but certain things caught my eye. One entire wall was taken up by a window, draped with delicate white curtains that reached the floor. In the corners of the window, heavy gold-brown curtains hung, thick and rich in texture. The only furniture besides the bed was a large built-in wardrobe, nearly three meters wide. The wooden dresser was finished with tiny golden flecks that shimmered in the light. Small lanterns stood on the floor, just like the ones scattered throughout the rest of the house.

The air was filled with the scent of wood, soon joined by the soothing aroma of lavender incense that Max had lit. The absence of rugs or carpets struck me as unusual—most people liked to have something soft to step onto when getting out of bed. But here, there were none. Max smelled the same as when I first met him, only stronger now. Even his sweat carried a faintly sweet scent.

When we finally decided to regain control of ourselves, we started talking about our next meeting. He suggested a trip to the river and even told me to bring Adam along. But I wasn't sure if it was too soon. My son had endured just as many painful memories as I had, except he was still just a little boy. I wanted him to have peace now, to avoid any overwhelming experiences for a while. Still, the idea of a trip felt warmer and more personal than just another date.

Lying in Max's arms, we planned our next outing—a picnic and a night under the open sky. He would pick the location because I had no idea where to go. I loved nature, but over the years, I had forgotten where the best places by the water were in our area. It was still hard for me to plan something for the future. It felt strange knowing that someone genuinely wanted to spend time with me. But thankfully, that feeling was starting to change.

As we talked, Max's fingers gently traced over my skin, occasionally pressing soft kisses to my forehead, sending shivers down my spine. I wasn't used to this kind of attention. He treated me as if I were the most delicate person in the world. Every touch, every movement was carefully thought out. The fact that someone could care for me in such a kind and responsible way both amazed and terrified me.

"Where are you sneaking off to?" Max asked, his voice low and teasing. "I need to check my phone," I replied, slipping on his shirt over my bare skin and tossing my hair back in one swift motion. Max caught my hand and kissed it, as if afraid I might never return. In the hallway, I spotted my small purse lying on the floor. Somehow, it had spilled open, scattering everything inside—including my phone. I picked it up and glanced at the screen: 8:12 a.m. Two messages. Both from Matilda. One sent around three in the morning, the other just five minutes ago. Quickly, I unlocked my phone and read them. It's almost 3:00 a.m.! Adam is sleeping soundly. I envy you! Take care of yourself. M. The next one was just as sweet: My dear friend, your little one is still sleeping peacefully and doing great. I can tell you're having a wonderful time! You have so much to tell me! Tonight—just you, me, and a bottle of wine! I want every detail. Let me know you're alive! M.

At that moment, I realized how much I could always count on her—and that tonight, I definitely wouldn't be getting much sleep. My best friend would make sure I didn't leave out a single detail from this date. I thought for a second and sent her a reply. I didn't want her to worry. I'm at Max's place. Everything is absolutely perfect! Last night was so eventful that I could tell you about it for days, not just one evening! P.S. For the next date, I might need a whole wagon of condoms, not just one! Alice."

I smiled to myself as I hit send. "Sweetheart, are you still there? Don't make me wait any longer, "I heard Max's voice calling from the bedroom. I tucked my phone into my purse and slung it over the back of one of the armchairs in the living room. Then, quickly, I made my way back to the bedroom. Max looked so happy that I almost felt guilty telling him I'd have to leave soon. Our time together had already stretched hours longer than I had planned. I hadn't intended to come home at dawn. "I'm here!" I called out, playfully jumping onto the edge of the bed before landing right on top of him, pressing a soft kiss to his lips. Max pulled his hands from under the blanket and ran them along my body again. "Thank you, Alice. For a wonderful evening, an incredible night, and a perfect morning. I could definitely get used to this," he said, brushing a strand of hair behind my ear.

"This was the best date of my life! Thank you! I actually wanted to ask you something... " I propped myself up slightly, looking closely at his face. "I'm listening," he said. "Tell me... was it good for you? Did I satisfy you? I didn't go out with you just for this, but I know I'm not very experienced... I'm probably way behind in all this and"—Max didn't let me finish. He silenced me with a deep, passionate kiss, just like the one he gave me in the pool last night.

"You are my ultimate fantasy come true," he murmured against my lips. "I don't even know if there's a phrase for this, but that's what I think. I could make love to you always, anywhere, anytime. I've never experienced anything like this with another woman. Look… " He grabbed my hand and placed it over his crotch. I felt just how much our conversation had affected him. We both burst into quiet laughter. Max suddenly flipped me onto my back and started tickling me, his fingers dancing across my skin. It felt so playful, so light, that I couldn't stop smiling.

After another hour in bed, we finally decided to have breakfast in the garden. Max prepared fresh sandwiches and boiled soft eggs. We sat at a small white folding table, enjoying our meal. Then, we shared a cup of espresso from his coffee machine. It was exquisite—the same kind I loved at work. The sight of Max, sitting there in nothing but his underwear and an unbuttoned shirt draped over his shoulders, was almost too much to handle. He looked so effortlessly sexy, so perfectly at ease. I wished I could see him like this every day.

Every now and then, he ran his fingers through his tousled hair or wiped his mouth with the back of his hand. Occasionally, he gazed at me with such intense interest that I started to wonder if he was even listening to what I was saying. He was both ruggedly masculine and irresistibly charming at the same time. I had spent an incredible evening, night, and morning with him. And now, one question remained in my mind. What happens next?

Alice sat across from me, wearing my white shirt from last night. Only two buttons were fastened, just enough to cover her breasts. She looked so unbelievably sexy that I had to fight the urge to throw her onto the lounge chair beside us or pull her into the pool. Her hair cascaded over her delicate collarbones, and she held a large golden coffee mug in her hands.

An idea struck me. Without saying a word, I got up and walked toward the living room, leaving her momentarily puzzled. I grabbed my mirrorless camera from the cabinet and returned to the table. I took so many pictures that I could have filled an entire album. I couldn't take my eyes off her.

Alice didn't hesitate—she smiled softly, shifting her gaze between me and the distance. In an instant, the woman I had just spent the night with transformed into a stunning model. After about fifteen minutes of snapping photos, she suddenly grinned and stuck her tongue out at me. We both burst into laughter, and I managed to capture that moment too.

At that moment, my camera became one of the most valuable things in my house. As we finished breakfast and the last sips of coffee, I asked her what time she wanted to head home. I had already planned to drive her safely back in my other car. I also offered her the use of my bathroom. I wasn't sure if she'd find it rude, but I figured it was best to ask. A woman who had just spent the night in my bed might appreciate a moment of privacy.

"I'll use your bathroom… but only if you join me," she said, setting her mug down and resting her face in her hands, elbows propped on the white table. "Of course! Any extra time with you is a pleasure," I replied, winking at her. I gathered the dishes and loaded them into the dishwasher, while Alice grabbed a yellow cloth from the kitchen handle and wiped down the table in the garden.

As soon as she finished, I took her hand and pulled her inside with me. My bathroom was upstairs, accessible via sturdy wooden stairs. I hoped she'd like the look of this room as much as the rest of the house. On the way, I grabbed clean towels for both of us. When we entered, I drew back the curtains and placed the towels neatly on a shelf beside the marble sink. "Damn, next time, we're sleeping in this bathtub! This place is amazing!" she exclaimed.

Hearing her say next time made me smile to myself. "Anywhere you want, we can sleep," I said, turning to face her, only to be met with her playful, flirtatious smile. Alice let my shirt slip off her shoulders and stepped toward me. Once again, she stood before me, completely naked, and began undressing me as well. She suddenly seemed fragile, delicate. I could tell that, standing here with me now, she wanted me to take care of her. I held her hand with one of mine and used the other to start filling the large bathtub in the center of the bathroom. Before the water had even reached the right level, she climbed in, sitting down slowly and looking at me expectantly. I joined her, and she leaned her back against my chest.

Worried that she might feel my arousal again, I quickly changed the subject. "How's your little boy doing?" I asked. "He's great, spending time with the best aunt in the world. He's been sleeping better these past few days, he's healthy and smiling. That's all I need," she replied with a warm smile.

We enjoyed a long, relaxing bath together. I used a large blue sponge to wash her entire body, and then she did the same for me. I felt so comfortable with her that I forgot about any insecurities I had. I stopped worrying about whether I looked good naked or if I should be self-conscious. I noticed she felt the same—she wasn't covering her scar anymore, she blushed less, and she kissed me first more often. I loved the thought that we were growing closer, opening up to each other more and more. Though, given the situation we were in, I wasn't sure how much more we could open up.

It occurred to me that Alice probably didn't have anything to wear. After all, we hadn't planned for her to stay the night. I wrapped her in a towel and led her back to my bedroom. I found an old tank top of mine, which had become too small for me, and a pair of my sister's athletic shorts, which I hadn't seen her wear in ages. We laughed for ten minutes at how her elegant heels absolutely did not match the casual outfit. Unfortunately, we had no other option.

Alice pulled a small glass perfume bottle from her purse and spritzed it on her collarbones. Then, turning to me, she extended the bottle in my direction. I didn't move—I wanted to smell her scent on me instead. The way she smiled after doing it made my heart swell. She climbed into my car and fastened her seatbelt. We talked the entire drive about all the things we wanted to do together and places we could go.

I was curious about her studies in floristry, so I asked her all about it. I was impressed. Until now, I had never thought of flower arrangements as someone's job. Florist shops had always just been there to me, and I had never considered how much skill and effort went into it. Now, I saw her work in a completely new light—it was both an art and a labor of love.

I parked the car right by the road and went out to open her door. The happiness in her eyes was overwhelming. I almost lost control and pulled her into a kiss right there in the middle of the street. It would have been childish for a grown man like me to be so impatient. But my emotions got the best of me. I pulled her into my arms, placed my hands on her waist, and kissed her deeply. She didn't move—she wanted it just as much as I did.

"See you later, Max," she said, flashing a warm smile. "Text me when your home, let me know Adam is okay. I'll call you tonight. And thank you for the perfume, maybe it'll help me not miss you too much," I said, pressing a kiss to her forehead. I walked back to the driver's side of the car and waited until she stepped inside her home. I had to. I needed to be sure she was safe.

As soon as she disappeared around the corner, I felt a tightness in my stomach. I already missed her. And it wasn't just her body, her kisses, or her touch. I missed our conversations, her laughter. In just a few days, she became my best friend, my anchor. All afternoon, I kept glancing at my phone, waiting for a message. Finally, at around 2:00 p.m., I read her text: Adam is doing great. I feel like he didn't even notice I was gone all night and morning. Now I have a very long conversation ahead of me with Matilda—there's no one more curious than her! Hope you make it home safely. I'll be waiting for your call tonight.

A wide grin spread across my face. We talked on the phone all evening. She told me everything she had to do that day and described, in real time, the funny antics of her son. Before I knew it, we had been talking for three hours. We settled on our next date—Friday evening, for a picnic. Her best friend would look after Adam again, and I'd have another chance to make her feel even happier than before.

It wasn't just about getting to know her anymore. It wasn't just about loving her. I had made it my mission to bring back her happiness. Ever since our night together, I knew I could do it. I was sure of it. It was still too early to say it out loud, but deep down, I was certain— I wanted Alice to be mine. Only mine.

The days leading up to Friday dragged on endlessly. All I had were our phone conversations to keep me going. I didn't want to be too pushy—I knew Alice had a child, a job, and was still recovering from traumatic experiences. I had to respect that. I spent the last few days of the week at work, trying to keep my mind occupied, to worry less, to distract myself. It didn't always work, but I really put in the effort.

As the weekend approached, I did everything I could to plan the perfect date. I picked Alice up around six in the evening from the same spot where we had last met. She was wearing tight denim shorts and a simple white t-shirt. On her feet, she had a pair of white Converse sneakers. I had never seen her dressed so casually, and she looked absolutely adorable. She was perfect—just right for me.

Before heading out, I had thrown on a loose white shirt with small Hawaiian patterns, leaving a few buttons undone, paired with black casual shorts and my own sneakers—though slightly different from hers. We looked like a real couple, ready for an evening picnic by the water.

I chose a lake outside the city, one that wasn't too crowded—not with elderly dog walkers, nor with rowdy teenagers. The water was surrounded by a tall forest, and every now and then, there were small, secluded beaches just big enough for a blanket, some lounge chairs, or even a small grill. I packed large string lights with a jute rope, a small radio, and a thick, soft blanket. In my portable cooler, I had a chilled bottle of white wine, some snacks, and ice cream.

When Alice got into my car, she greeted me with a kiss on the cheek. "Hi! I don't know about you, but I've been counting down the days to this!" she said, turning to me with excitement. "Me too. I've missed you so—" I started, but she cut me off. I meant the picnic! she teased, then let out a soft giggle. I joined in, shaking my head with a smile.

During the twenty-minute drive to the lake, I casually reached for her hand a few times, resting it on my knee. We picked up some unfinished conversations—one about her new keto diet, which quickly turned into a shared realization that we both loved food too much to stick to any restrictive eating plan. We agreed that we'd enjoy everything in moderation—at any time of day—though that might not be the best for our fitness in the long run. But we also talked about staying active. We both enjoyed swimming, long walks, and even hitting the gym. So, any extra pounds we might gain, we'd work off together.

When we arrived, we took a stroll along the lake, walking about half a kilometer into the forest before we found a perfect sunlit, secluded little beach. "This looks like the perfect spot," I said, setting down the blanket. "Yeah, I think so too!" Alice agreed, nodding in approval.

As I unpacked everything we had brought, Alice slipped off her white sneakers, leaving them neatly by the blanket, and walked toward the water's edge. She turned back to me, waving me over with a playful smile. I hadn't even been with her for an hour, and I already felt like the luckiest man alive. She looked so effortlessly beautiful, as if she was born for moments like this. Her outfit, her smile, the way her ponytail swayed slightly in the breeze—everything about her was perfect. Not wanting to waste a second, I kicked off my own shoes and followed her.

Alice suddenly splashed some water in my direction with her hands. On a warm day like this, a few cool drops were actually refreshing. But I wasn't about to let her win that easily. Without hesitation, I grabbed her by the waist and playfully led her further into the water. Our laughter echoed across the lake, and for a moment, I forgot my own name. Her wet clothes clung to her body, accentuating her perfect figure. Droplets of water ran down the strands of her hair, making her look even more radiant. She was already a graceful woman I couldn't resist, a strong and caring mother. But now, she was also a carefree girl, splashing in the lake, full of joy and lightness.

As the evening set in, the sun started to dip lower, its reflection shimmering beautifully on the water's surface. I opened the bottle of white wine and poured it into two transparent glasses, each wrapped with a small golden ribbon I had tied earlier. I had paid attention to every little detail of this evening.

As always, our conversation flowed effortlessly—one topic leading to another, never a moment of awkward silence. For most of the night, we lounged on the striped picnic blanket, soaking in the scenery and each other's company. Up until now, I had only allowed myself a few small romantic gestures. I didn't want to rush things. Just having her beside me was enough. We didn't need to do anything more. But as I watched her face, glowing in the warm evening light, I could no longer fight my urges. I reached out and gently traced my fingers along her cheek. And in that moment, only one thought filled my mind—one that made me laugh at myself. I was a grown man, but being with Alice made me feel like a teenager.

"Alice, there's something I want to ask you," I said cautiously, but I don't know where to start. 'I suggest starting from the beginning," she replied with a teasing smile, hugging her knees to her chest, waiting for me to continue. "We haven't known each other for long—I know that. I know about your struggles, and you know about mine. I want to keep discovering you, day after day. And I want you to feel safe. Truly safe," I said, my gaze drifting to the water for a moment before I looked back at her. This time, I held her hand more firmly. I also want you to trust me. I know this is a lot, and that everything between us has been fast and intense—"

Before I could finish, Alice placed her hands on my face, stopping me. "Max… are you trying to ask if I'll be your girlfriend? Or are you about to reject me?" she asked in a playful tone, instantly breaking the tension. We both burst into laughter. She knew exactly how to turn an emotional moment into something light and joyful. "Yes," I admitted, smiling. "That's exactly what I wanted to ask. Will you be with me? Will you let me stand by your side? By your side, by Adam's side? I accept every part of you. You don't have to be afraid—I will always protect you, and I will do my best never to let you down."

As I spoke, I saw a smile spread across her lips— But at the same time, a single tear rolled down her cheek. Without hesitation, I wiped it away with my thumb. She looked so fragile in that moment, just like she did from time to time when her emotions overwhelmed her. With me, she could feel whatever she wanted. And I knew, from this moment on— I would always be there for her.

I loved this evening. The silence, the peace, the perfect company. I finally stopped worrying, and I felt my strength returning. I think it was because of him. He helped me get back on my feet, reminded me that I was still alive, and that it was time to wake up from this nightmare. I needed to pull myself together, find a new place to live, and get a better job. Somehow, I would manage—I had to. Max believed in me. Everything would be okay.

As we sat under the moonlight, holding hands, my phone suddenly vibrated. I glanced at the screen and saw three missed calls from Matilda. Something must have happened! "What's wrong?" Max asked, his voice full of concern. "I have no idea. I need to call her back." I was immediately on edge, and only one thought crossed my mind—something had happened to Adam. In an instant, I was on my feet, dialing Matilda's number. I didn't have to wait long for her to pick up. "Alice, damn it!

I've been calling you over and over!" she yelled into the phone, not even giving me a chance to speak. This had to be serious.

"A police officer just called me—someone is outside Max's house, screaming at the top of his lungs that he's going to set it on fire! He's got a gas can and a lighter! It's a nightmare! The officer said it's probably Olaf! What kind of connections do you have with the police? Why are they calling me? What the hell do I do? Where are you? Hello?!" Matilda was panicked, and rightfully so. My stomach dropped.
"Matilda, watch over Adam. No one except me is allowed into the house, do you understand? I'll call you back, I said firmly." "Alice, but what are you going to do?! Of course, I'll take care of Adam, don't worry, but what if—," she started, but I cut her off. There was no time for explanations. I ended the call and shoved my phone into my bag. A lump formed in my throat. My whole body froze.

Then, I felt Max's presence behind me, his warm breath on my neck. His hands rested gently on my shoulders. "What happened? Say something!" His voice was tense. "Olaf wants to burn down your house," I finally managed to say. "Your friend couldn't reach you, so he found Matilda's number and called her." Saying it out loud made it feel even more terrifying. "What the hell?!" Max's voice filled with anger. I could hear the rage bubbling inside him. "Max, this is all my fault," I whispered, my voice cracking. "Take me there. To your house. I'll fix this. I'll talk to him, I don't know, something. Just take me there."

I frantically started packing up our things. "Alice, stop for a second! Look at me!" Max grabbed my arms, his voice firm. "You are not fixing anything. Did you hear what I said earlier? Not long ago? I meant it. I'm taking care of you. I won't let you go back to him, and I sure as hell won't let anything happen to you! Do you understand me? Listen to what I'm saying. We're leaving. I'm taking you to Matilda's, then I'll deal with this." "No way! You are not going there alone! I dragged you into this mess—I'm coming with you!" I snapped.

There was no time to argue. We packed up quickly and rushed toward Max's house. I had only known him for a short time, and yet this was the second time I had seen him so tense. And it was all because of me. How could I possibly let him face this alone? That wasn't an option. The entire car ride was spent in silence. He didn't say a word, and neither did I. Every now and then, he'd take my hand, kiss it, or place it on his knee—just like he always did. But I was too anxious to find any comfort in it. All the happiness of the past few days had evaporated, as if it had never even existed. Would Olaf always ruin my life? Not just mine, but Max's too? And Adam's? And Matilda's?

As we neared Max's house, I spotted two police cars parked outside. Four officers stood nearby. Three of them I recognized instantly were the same ones who had rescued me from Olaf before. We pulled into the driveway. Almost every house on the street had their porch lights on, and curious neighbors were peering out from their windows. Max yanked the handbrake, unfastened his seatbelt in one quick motion, and reached for the door handle—but then he hesitated. "Stay here," he ordered. "You wanted to come, so you did. But we don't have time to argue about what we should or shouldn't do. Stay in the car. Do it for me." He pressed a quick kiss to my forehead before stepping out, not giving me a chance to protest.

Why did I let him go alone? I watched as he approached the front yard, but the police car next to us blocked most of my view. Thankfully, it started rolling forward, giving me a clear line of sight to the driveway, the front entrance, and the pathway leading to the backyard. Olaf stood on the porch steps, surrounded by officers. Max walked toward him, picking up speed. He pushed through the officers, who didn't even try to stop him, and started speaking to Olaf, his fists clenched.

I felt like I was trapped in a horror movie. I had no idea what to do. Run? Hide? Attack Olaf myself. With shaking hands, I unlocked the car door and cracked the window open slightly. I would be lying if I said I wasn't terrified. I was. But I was even more afraid of something happening to Max—because of me. Olaf was shorter than Max, almost looking like a child next to him. He wasn't strong or muscular, but that didn't mean he wasn't dangerous. He was unpredictable. Seeing him now—his wild gestures, the way he destroyed everything around him—I wondered how I had lived with him for so long. He was completely unhinged. Alcohol and drugs had rotted his brain. There was no saving him.

"I'm asking you nicely—leave my property," Max said, his voice calm but firm. "I'm not going anywhere. I'll burn this dump to the ground," Olaf spat, pulling a cigarette and a lighter from his pocket. Instantly, every officer tensed. So, did Max. "I'm asking one last time—walk away. Oh, I'll walk away—but not without her. Let Alice get out of that car and send her to me. Then, maybe we'll skip the bonfire," Olaf sneered, lighting his cigarette. "You're pathetic," Max growled. "You lost your family, and this is how you try to get back at her? Be a man, for fuck's sake!"

Max was fuming now, his fists clenched so tightly that veins popped out on his forearms. I couldn't take it anymore. I unbuckled my seatbelt, pushed the door open, and rushed toward the house. "Alice, get back in the car!" Max turned to me, pointing at the vehicle. Coward, Olaf sneered—and then whack. He hit Max. Hard. I had no idea what he used, but Max fell to his knees. I froze. Why had I left the car? Max had promised he'd handle it. I only made things worse. I tried to run to him, but an officer grabbed me by the waist, holding me back. Max got back up. "I'm not fighting you," Max said, straightening himself. "I won't dirty my hands with you. Officers handle this."

But Olaf wanted a fight. "You screw the biggest whore in town, and you won't dirty your hands with me?" Olaf spat on the pavement. Something inside Max snapped. "You're done," Max said. And then—boom. One punch. Then another. Olaf crumpled to the ground. Max turned toward me, breathing

heavily, and started walking my way— Then—"GET DOWN!"
A deafening explosion. The sky lit up in flames. Olaf had done
it. That lunatic had set Max's house on fire.

I had no idea how long I would lay on the pavement.
The moment the explosion sent debris flying toward me, I
collapsed. But as soon as I could, I forced myself to get up. The
only thing on my mind was Alice. Was she okay? I could hear
sirens wailing in the distance, the sound of firefighters rushing
in. My house was in flames. From a quick glance, the damage
didn't seem catastrophic, but none of that mattered right now.
Through the crowd and the thick dust hanging in the air, I
struggled to push my way toward the car—where I had last
seen her.

People stopped me, asking over and over, Are you okay?!
But I ignored them. I didn't have time to answer. It felt like I
had run miles, even though my car was parked right in my
driveway. I turned my head repeatedly, scanning the chaos,
afraid I had somehow missed Alice lying somewhere in the
wreckage. Then, finally, by my neighbor's mailbox, I saw her.
She was standing with my friend, and he was holding onto her
tightly—too tightly. I realized she must have tried to run toward
me.

The moment our eyes met; I felt a massive weight lift
from my chest. I was so overwhelmed with relief that my eyes
burned with unshed tears. Alice broke free from my friend's
grip and ran at me, jumping into my arms. She clung to me so
tightly I could barely breathe, her legs wrapped around my
waist, her fingers tangled in my hair. We must have looked like
something out of an action movie. Without thinking, I covered
her face with kisses—her forehead, her cheeks, her lips. I didn't
need anything else in this world. "Are you okay? Max, are you
okay?" she practically screamed into my ear. "I'm fine, love.
I swear, I'm fine. Are you okay?" I asked, my voice was thick
with emotion. I'm fine, she nodded. I just don't know how your
friend managed to hold me back with so much force, she added

with a small, breathless laugh before pressing her lips to mine again. I finally set her down, keeping her close.

We started walking toward the car, but my friend's voice suddenly stopped me. "Max! Wait!" I turned to him immediately. "That bastard ran off," he said. "Luckily, the damage isn't as bad as it looks. The loudest explosion came from a gas canister Olaf had with him. Inside the house, nothing major is destroyed. You'll need to fix the windows, the front door, and part of the roof, but—" "It doesn't matter, I cut him off. I'll deal with it later. "But listen—find a way to lock him up for good. I don't care how. He's dangerous. If this were just about me, you know I could handle it. But it's not just about me anymore." I glanced at Alice, pulling her closer to me. My friend nodded. "I get it. I'll do my best. We'll stay in touch." And with that, he disappeared into the crowd of neighbors.

I suddenly realized that before everything settled down, I needed to figure out where to stay. To stay somewhere, I needed to pack a few things. And to stay for more than a few days, I needed to take some extra cash. I tightened my grip on Alice's hand and turned back toward the house. She didn't ask any questions, she knew exactly what I was thinking. We entered through the back garden and made our way to my bedroom. I threw a few essentials into a bag, along with an envelope of cash from my drawer. I wasn't a millionaire, but I had plenty of savings, a solid income, and no financial worries. I could take care of myself, help my sister, spoil Alice with jewelry every day if I wanted to, and still not worry about checking my bank balance. I also packed my camera. I didn't know if I'd ever be able to part with it.

When we returned to the car, I looked at Alice and could tell she wanted to say something. "Max, I... I don't know what to say. I'm so sorry. Your beautiful house... this is all my fault. I dragged my problems onto you. What am I supposed to do now? There's only one solution—I have to go back. I'd rather let him hurt me than risk him hurting the people I love." She dropped her face into her hands. For the first time, I heard her truly sob. Without thinking, I unbuckled my seatbelt and reached for her hands, pulling them away from her face. "Baby, this is not your fault. None of this is your fault. And tonight, I realized something—if anything happened to you, it would break me. I'm crazy about you. I'll protect you, no matter what, no matter who I must fight. Do you hear me?" Her hands trembled in mine, and she covered her face again. "I didn't want to say this now, in these circumstances. I didn't want to say it so soon. We're adults. I haven't even met your son yet, and I wanted to wait. But now… in this moment, I can't hold it in anymore." Alice loosened her hands slightly but didn't fully uncover her face. "I love you. Do you understand? I love you. With or without problems. Yesterday, today, tomorrow. I knew it days ago, but tonight, when I lost sight of you in that chaos—I knew. This is real. And I will say it and show it to you as many times as it takes. Do you hear me, Alice?" I surprised even myself with the certainty in my voice.

Alice slowly pulled her hands away from her face, placing them on her lap. "Max, I… I love you too," she whispered. What we had just confessed wasn't a fleeting moment of passion, it was a promise. I hadn't said it in bed. I hadn't said it over a romantic dinner. I had said it after the most terrifying night of our lives. Tonight, I had felt the real possibility of losing her. Losing her to that toxic home she had escaped. Losing her in the fire Olaf had set. The thought stabbed me in the heart. I had only known her for two months, yet I couldn't imagine life without her. It was like an addiction—I thought about her every day, every night. I could watch her forever. I memorized every smile. And her touch? It drove me insane. I never thought love would hit me like this. But just as quickly as I had found happiness with her, it felt like it was slipping away.

"Max," Alice broke the silence, "we can't see each other anymore. I can't put you in danger like this. Baby— Max, I can't be with you. Do you understand?" She suddenly opened the car door and stepped outside. "I would die if something happened to you. Do you understand? If I could understand you, then you must understand me!" Her last words came out as a scream. Before I could react, she was already five steps away, heading toward the bus stop. I didn't know whether to chase after her or let her go. One thing was clear—I had opened my heart to her. But I couldn't force her to stay. I had Matilda's number. I would reach out soon, ask her if Alice got home safely. Maybe she just needed space. And honestly, I couldn't blame her.

I checked into a hotel not far from my house—somewhere different this time. I didn't want to impose on Alice. I hadn't even reached my room when my phone vibrated. Matilda. She had responded to my message: "Alice is with me. She's already asleep. She looked awful, and I heard her crying. I don't know how to help her. But anyway, she's safe with me, and I won't let anything happen to her. M." It was the only thing that had given me any sense of relief since arriving at the hotel. Alice was safe. Nothing else mattered.

The days dragged on unbearably. I thought I was losing my mind. I checked my phone constantly. Silence. I drowned myself in extra work, took on additional projects, and started the repairs on my house. But no matter what I did, I couldn't focus. All I could see in my mind was her. The way she had looked at me, her eyes filled with tears, telling me she had to leave. Because that's what I understood—she was leaving me. My heart still beats for her, but frustration and helplessness consumed me. A week has passed. Then another. I missed Alice so much that I started sleeping in the T-shirt she had worn, the one still carrying her scent. I wasn't eating properly. I wasn't sleeping. Day and night blended into one long, miserable blur. I was completely shattered. On the 43rd day since I last saw Alice, I finally gave in. I sent her a message. That's enough time, I told myself. I had fought the urge every day, resisting the temptation to call or text her. But I finally broke. "Let me still be in your life. Let me still be your friend. Max." I had no idea why I sent such a pathetic, pointless message. It wasn't what I wanted. Not at all. Within five minutes, she replied. "Friends. Great idea. Have a nice day, friend. Alice."

Reading it didn't make me feel any better. From what I had gathered, Alice was still living with Matilda. Olaf had disappeared—possibly fled the country. And me? I was stuck. For the next two weeks, Alice ignored my calls and messages. And I was drowning. I felt like I was spiraling downward. I couldn't take it anymore. I had to see her. She had to talk to me. I threw on the first clothes I could find, grabbed my keys, and headed to the underground parking garage. My Mercedes was parked on the top floor, so it took me almost fifteen minutes just to exit the hotel. I reached Matilda's apartment in twenty minutes. My hands were sweaty. My heart was pounding in my chest. I typed out a message to Alice: "I'm downstairs. Please come down. Max." And then, I waited. I would wait as long as it took.

But I didn't have to wait long. From around the corner, I saw her. She was wearing black sweatpants and a white T-shirt, her arms crossed under her chest. I didn't get out of the car this time. Maybe I was scared. She opened the door and slipped into the passenger seat. "Hey," she greeted me softly. "It's good to see you." I let out a slow breath. "Thank you for coming." Then, I couldn't stop myself. "Why haven't you answered me? You don't pick up, you don't reply… Are you okay?" I instinctively reached toward her knee—but stopped myself just in time. She noticed. "I didn't want to," she admitted. "I had to end this somehow… to protect you." Her words warmed my heart. "You know we don't have to end this," I said quietly. Alice dropped her gaze, staring at the floor of my car.

Chapter 10

Choosing a Different Life

"My mother was right," I whisper softly. "Alice, speak clearly, please. I don't understand why you can't just say what you mean. I thought that even after rejecting my proposal, we could still be friends... Please, at least let me be in your life this way," Max responds, confused. "My mother was right...," I started again; my voice was barely audible as I stared at the car floor. "She was right! I finally understood what she meant. I know now what love looks like. I thought it would never happen to me." We sit in silence for a while, staring at the dim glow of the car's radio as Celine Dion's My Heart Will Go On plays.

I hadn't seen his face, smelled his scent, or felt his touch in so long. And now, sitting beside him, I feel like I'm losing my mind. This is my man. I love him just as much as he loves me. Yet I can't allow us to be happy. I must let him go. I couldn't bear to live with the thought that something terrible might happen to him because of me.

"Baby, look at me," Max suddenly says. He reaches out and cups my face. "I love you", he adds. "Give us a chance. Give me a chance. And don't worry about me. Being with you makes me the happiest man on earth." "Max, you still don't understand, do you?" I shake my head, my voice trembling. "I'm just a hotel maid. I was beaten and raped for five years. I live with my child at my best friend's house. My ex tried to burn down the house of the man I sleep with and the man I love. And you don't see anything wrong with that?!" I take a deep breath and continue, my voice breaking. "I absorbed everything bad from Olaf, like a sponge. And now, all of it is falling on you—an innocent man. I love you too, just as much as you love me... And that's why I want to protect you."

"Stop talking nonsense." Max's voice is firm. "Before I even spoke to you at that bus stop, I already knew about your problems. And I still chose to go forward. This isn't just your decision, Alice—it's mine too!" I feel utterly powerless. Max takes my hands and places them on his face. "Alice. Do you see me?" he asks. "Yes," I whisper. "I love you. The only way you could destroy my life is by leaving me. Do you understand?" I broke. I'm not just torturing myself—I'm torturing him. I've talked about this a million times with Matilda. She never judged me for pushing him away, but even she didn't understand where Max found the strength and patience to keep fighting for me.

I remember the fire. I remember looking into his eyes that night. There was no fear of losing his house, only fear of losing me. I had never seen anything like that before. His love for me was so overwhelming, and that's what made all this so hard. We sat in silence for nearly ten minutes. Max presses his forehead against mine, his hands gently cradling my tear-streaked face. Every now and then, he wipes my tears or kisses my nose. "It's okay now, baby. Everything is okay. Just breathe," Max soothes me.

"It's all happening too fast. I can't keep up. I'm so sorry for everything," I whisper. "I know it's fast," he says gently. "But is there a set time for falling in love? Is there a rule that tells us when we're allowed to love someone? There isn't. It just happens. And now, we have two choices: we either stand up and fight together, or we spend the rest of our lives regretting what we lost." Tears well up in my eyes again. "What do we do now?" I ask.

"I'm staying in a hotel for now," Max explains. "My house is being repaired, but luckily, the damage isn't too bad. Olaf has disappeared, and my friend hasn't been able to track him down yet. If he resurfaces, they'll lock him up for years for what he's already done—and for what he tried to do to us. I'll find a good lawyer to make sure everything is handled properly." He continues, his voice steady, full of certainty. "Once my house is ready—it'll probably take another month—we'll set up a room for your son. And when you're ready, you'll move in with me. No pressure. Until then, I'll plan the best dates for us. Maybe we can even start looking for a space to open your own little flower shop? I know it's a lot to take in at once. But I think keeping ourselves busy will help. No more worrying. I just want us to be happy. Let's not waste any more time."

The conviction in his voice is so strong, it convinces me, too. "I don't know how you do it," I whisper. "You're so optimistic. I've missed that." Max smiles softly. "I'm not here just to take you on dates, bring you flowers, or make love to you—though, I'll admit, that last part is my favorite." I let out a shaky laugh. "I want to help you stand on your own feet again. I never want to lose you ever again, Alice. These past weeks without you… I thought my heart would break." This time, I kissed him. A deep, slow, passionate kiss. We talked for a little while longer, then I started to leave the car. "I'll see you tomorrow. I'll come pick you up. Take care of yourself, please," Max says. I pause. Before I can think, I blurt out: "What do you think about a children's play center? Max, would you like to meet my son?" A flicker of surprise flashes across his face. "Are you serious?" he asks. I nodded. "Of course, I'd love to," he beams." I'll pick you both up at three. Choose the place, and we'll go."

Max steps out of the car and walks over to open my door. He pulls me into a tight hug. "I love you. Give your son a kiss from me," he whispers in my ear before kissing my forehead. "I will. Text me when you get to the hotel safely," I say softly. The words don't come easily. I rarely say them. But this time…"I love you, Max. Goodnight." And it feels so easy.

I spent half the night choosing the perfect place for my son to play. I was so excited about this meeting that I almost ran out of time getting ready. I put on the most comfortable clothes I could find and did the same for Adam. Today was going to be a great day. My son woke up in a good mood, which meant everything was off to a good start. All afternoon, I worried about how Max would interact with my child. I had never even asked if he liked kids or if he ever thought about having his own. Accepting someone else's child isn't an easy thing. But if he wanted to be with me, he had to love my son too. I had never been in this kind of situation before. The thought of it made my throat tighten.

At exactly three o'clock, I heard the honk of a car outside. I peeked through the window and saw Max leaning against the passenger door, holding his phone. I knew immediately who he was calling. I picked up. "Good morning, sweetheart. Are you ready? Should I come up? Need help with anything? You look beautiful!" He lifted his hand in a wave as he spoke. "Good morning. No need, we'll be right down!" I replied. I picked up Adam and swung our bag over my shoulder. In my other hand, I carried the car seat. It was a lot to carry, but I wanted Max to see that I could handle everything on my own. The moment he saw me, he ran toward me. "What are you doing?! Don't you know that's what men are for? Carrying things!" He teased, kissing me gently before turning to my son. "Hey, buddy! How are you? Wow, you're so handsome!"

He took Adam's tiny hand in his and then looked back at me. "Alice, he looks exactly like you!" Then, to my surprise, Max placed a tender kiss on Adam's forehead. He studied him for a moment, his face full of wonder and a soft smile. "Shall we go?" I asked, breaking the silence. "Of course, I'll install the car seat right now," Max responded. He did it faster than I ever could. Then, to my surprise, he took Adam from my arms and carefully buckled him in. I was stunned. I hadn't expected him to handle everything so effortlessly. It might seem like a simple task, but when you're a parent, you notice these things.

The road to the play center was winding, making my son giggle almost the entire way. And when my child laughed, I laughed too. Max, of course, joined in. I had been looking forward to the moment they would finally meet. But even more, I was excited to spend time together as a family. I felt both happiness and nervous anticipation. But I also feared what would happen next. Would Max feel overwhelmed after spending time with us? Would he realize that, while he loves me, he could never love my son? I had no idea.

As we approached the play center, Max placed his hand on my knee again. "Sweetheart, how are you feeling? You're quieter than usual," he asked. "I'm fine… just a little nervous," I admitted, placing my hand over his. "Why? You can tell me anything," Max pressed gently. "I'm afraid this is too much for you all at once—me, my son, and everything that comes with us," I confessed, my voice barely above a whisper. Saying it out loud made it feel even more real.

Max unbuckled his seatbelt and turned to face me. "Sweetheart, I chose to spend today with you and your son. No one forced me to do this," he reassured me, pressing a soft kiss to my hand. The day turned out to be absolutely perfect. The smile never left Adam's face—not even for a second. And what surprised me the most? It never left mine or Max's either. I love taking care of my child, but today, Max practically took over for me. He ran around with Adam, played with him, climbed through the play structures, and made him laugh nonstop. It was perfect. All my worries about today completely disappeared.

It has been eleven months and four days since Alice and I officially became a couple. Time is flying by relentlessly. Yet every single day, I feel the same as I did when I first realized I loved her. Her smile is everything to me. The sound of Adam's laughter and the way we spend our quiet evenings together as a family—the three of us—make me the happiest man on earth. I never imagined I would have something like this. Day by day, I truly believe fate has written us a beautiful story. Our days are simple, yet so extraordinary. We share incredible moments together. We love each other, all three of us. Since Alice and Adam moved in with me, I no longer feel lonely. Waking up to Alice's beautiful face, inhaling her sweet scent, and tasting her kisses all day long has become my reality. Our intimacy became even more meaningful once we started living together. She felt safe, and I knew she was mine. That gave us incredible strength. Our life feels like a romance movie with the perfect cast. It's almost hard to believe that we made it.

For the past month, I've been planning something big. I want to propose to Alice. I've been wrestling with my thoughts, afraid she might say no. But I don't want to wait anymore. I'm thirty-six years old, madly in love, and truly happy. A few weeks ago, we had the most perfect night together. We planned a date night at home. Matilda took care of Adam so we could have time just for us. From the evening until late at night, we stayed in the pool, wrapped in each other's arms.Later, we moved to the living room, sipping wine by the fireplace while watching Wuthering Heights. Before heading to bed, we spent some time together in the oversized bathtub—where, as always, our emotions got the best of us. A beautiful night with the woman I love ended in our bedroom, in our bed. Everything was perfect. And the fact that I could now call it ours made it even better.

I loved every moment spent with my beloved, but I have to admit—I also loved spending time with Adam just as much. I love that child with all my heart. He may not be my biological son, but I treat him as if he were. I treat him with the same love and care as I do his mother. I respect Alice, but I admire her even more for being an incredible mother. When Adam is sick, I stay up all night with him. I pick him up from daycare, take him to the pool every Thursday afternoon, and play with him at the park. I would do anything for that boy.

Now that I have a plan for the proposal, I feel both excited and terrified. What if she says no? That would break my heart in half. I know Alice loves me. I know she and Adam are my everything. But when I get down on one knee and ask her to spend the rest of her life with me—what will she say? I know she's mine. She loves me, she's crazy about me, and I know she'll always be there. So why am I so nervous? Maybe I'm just losing my mind from all the stress.

I decided to propose to Alice on Christmas Eve. She loves the holiday season as much as I do. We had planned to celebrate together, just the three of us. Two weeks before Christmas, we decorated the entire house with lights, ornaments, and festive trinkets. We bought an enormous real Christmas tree and placed it in the corner of the living room between the fireplace and the window. We decorated it with gold and red accents and delicate white angels. It was beautiful. Through the windows, it shone so brightly that our jealous neighbors across the street might stop talking to us. We always had a little friendly rivalry when it came to holiday decorations. But this year, our house looked magical. It was clear that love filled every corner of it.

The engagement ring I chose for Alice was gold with a large diamond. I wanted it to look grand on her delicate hand. Honestly, she deserved an entire wagon of diamonds, not just one. I had it wrapped in a red velvet box, which I then covered in golden paper and sealed with a small red bow. Everything was ready. We had promised to exchange gifts after Adam went to sleep. Until then, we planned to focus entirely on him. We had picked out a few toys for him, and tonight was his night. But the night? The night would be ours.

We had an amazing Christmas dinner, which we definitely overdid. I love spending time in the kitchen with Alice. She looked stunning in her red apron with a reindeer on it. If Adam hadn't been there, I would have laid her down on the kitchen island and done exactly what I wanted with her. She was gorgeous—even with a white flour smudge on her stomach from the reindeer's nose. Underneath the apron, I could see a peek of the red lace from her sexy yet elegant dress.She wore the gold jewelry I had given her for her birthday. Her hair was styled in a loose bun, and her lips were painted with deep red lipstick. I had kissed her so many times that night, yet somehow, her lipstick still held up. I guess I'm a little behind when it comes to that sort of thing. Everything was perfect. All that was missing was the ring on her finger.

Adam fell asleep in the blink of an eye. Our playtime had been so intense that even Alice gracefully kicked off her shoes and curled up comfortably in the armchair by the fireplace. Despite the long day, she still looked just as stunning as she did in the morning. And then, the moment arrived. I reached for the small, gift-wrapped box I had tucked away in the dresser and walked toward her. Taking her hand, I gently led her closer to our beautifully lit Christmas tree. A genuine, radiant smile spread across her face—the kind I loved the most.

"My love, I have something for you," I said, kneeling down on one knee, holding the small box in one hand and her fingers in the other. Before speaking, I kissed her hand tenderly. "Alice, I met you by pure chance. I fell in love with you, and I keep falling in love with you every single day. I want to spend my life by your side. You are my entire world. Will you marry me?" Tears welled up in my eyes. "Max…" she whispered, her voice breaking as she burst into tears. "Yes! Of course, I will marry you!" Before I could react, she threw herself into my arms, clinging to me as she always did. We stood there, holding each other tightly for a long moment, and I almost forgot I was still holding the ring. I showered her face with kisses, wiping away her happy tears. Even with her eyes glistening, she looked absolutely breathtaking. Maybe because I knew these were tears of joy.

Will you try it on?"" I asked, leaning back slightly. "You know, engagement traditions require a ring to be on your finger." We both laughed. I handed her the tiny box, and she unwrapped it slowly, carefully lifting the lid. "Oh my God, Max! It's stunning! You must have spent a fortune! You didn't have to!" "Yes, I had to. You deserve so much more." She handed me the ring, and I slid it onto her finger. It fit perfectly—just as I had imagined. Once again, we melted into each other's arms.

I was the happiest man alive. Everything was falling into place, and it was only going to get better. Or at least, that's what I thought. That night was magical—it felt different, more extraordinary than ever before. We were engaged now. It was romantic, playful, and filled with laughter as we joked about our upcoming small wedding. Alice massaged my back, and I gave her a foot massage in return. Even though I had been married before, I had never experienced an engagement like this. With Victoria, we simply got married—no proposal, no anticipation. This time was different. I wanted this. I wanted to propose. I wanted the wedding. I wanted children. With her. It was extraordinary, yet felt so natural. We had already been living together, so the engagement felt like the perfect final touch—a cherry on top of the life we had built. That night, we even talked about expanding our family. I had never been afraid of responsibility. Even though I already treated Adam as my own, I wanted children of my own. A bigger family had always been one of my dreams. And one of those dreams—I held in my arms all night long.

The next morning I woke up before everyone else. I wanted to prepare breakfast. I started slicing tomatoes for a salad, boiled some eggs, and set the plates on the kitchen counter. But from the moment I got up, I had been feeling off. A strange tightness in my chest. I took a glass of cold water, hoping it would help. It didn't. I placed my hands on my throat, pressing against my lymph nodes. They felt swollen. A wave of heat surged through me. I brushed it off as nothing serious and continued preparing breakfast. Ten minutes later, I collapsed on the kitchen floor—right beside our kitchen island.

Chapter 11

Still Standing

I said Yes! It was one of the biggest days of my life! I didn't even hesitate for a second—my answer came straight from my heart. It was the most genuine response I had ever given anyone. I was so sure of my love for Max. And even more sure of him. He was everything I had ever been looking for. A wonderful man who cared for me, made me feel safe, and for the first time in my life, made me feel beautiful. In his eyes, I was the most amazing woman in the world—and that's exactly how I felt. We were perfect together. He was my best friend, the man I could spend endless days with, wrapped up in bed. And, to top it all off, he loved my son. That mattered just as much as what we felt for each other. We were already starting to feel like a family. But now? It was real.

A strange noise woke me up. I checked on Adam—thankfully, he was still sleeping peacefully. I threw on my favorite white robe—the one Max had given me for my birthday. It was soft, embroidered with delicate gold thread. On the back, in elegant lettering, it read: Mrs. Frans. One of the most thoughtful gifts I had ever received. I looked around the bedroom—Max wasn't there. I walked through the hallway and into the living room. Still no sign of him. Then, I made my way to the kitchen. I saw half-prepared vegetables on the counter, a few boiled eggs, neatly set mint-colored plates, and tall glasses. But then, I stepped forward and froze. Max was lying on the kitchen floor.

I had no idea what had happened—but it looked terrible.
I rushed over to him, trying to lift him up, but I wasn't strong
enough. I checked his head for any injuries, but there was nothing visible. I ran cold water over my hands and pressed them
against his forehead, calling his name over and over. Nothing.
I did it again. And again. Finally, after the third time, his eyes
barely started to open. I had no idea what to do. I sprinted to
the bedroom, grabbing my phone from the charger. On the
way, I threw open the front door and wedged a large glass vase
between the doorframe—the only thing I could find at that moment.
I dialed emergency services while rushing back to the kitchen.
A woman answered, asking me what had happened. I gave her
the shortest possible version—then yelled at her to send an ambulance immediately. I gave her the address, ended the call, and
ran back to Max. Waiting felt like an eternity. I sat on the cold
floor, leaning against the kitchen cabinets, cradling Max's face in
my hands. This was a nightmare. Our entire life flashed before
my eyes. Tears dripped down onto his shirt, one after another.
Max stared blankly, his eyes open, but he didn't seem fully con-
scious. He hadn't said a single word. Until suddenly…"I love
you," he whispered, before closing his eyes again. "I love you,
too. Don't move, baby. Just stay with me," I choked out, kissing
his forehead.

Then, I heard the sirens. I screamed as loud as I could,
waking Adam in the process—his cries now echoing from his
bedroom. I kept calling out to the paramedics, my voice trembling with tears. I heard them burst through the front door and
rush toward the kitchen. And then—everything started happening too fast. I couldn't breathe. The worst part? I wasn't allowed
to go with Max to the hospital. I had to stay home with Adam.
Two paramedics checked his pulse, flashed a small light into his
eyes. That's all I could remember. I clung to Max's hand, kissing
him over and over—his forehead, his fingers—desperately try-

ing to do something, anything. But what could I do? What was happening?

They lifted him onto the stretcher and wheeled him toward the ambulance. My entire world—my everything—was slipping away before my eyes. As they loaded him into the ambulance, I whispered, "I love you so much." He didn't answer. I don't even know if he heard me. As the ambulance sped away, I rushed inside, scooping Adam into my arms. I had no idea how long he had been awake, but thankfully, he was still safe in his crib. He was always such a good child. I grabbed my phone and called Matilda. I begged her to come over and watch Adam. I had to go. I had to be there with Max. I couldn't leave him alone. I had no idea what was wrong with him.

It was only 10 a.m., but Matilda had to leave work early. Luckily, she didn't live far. She was at my door within twenty minutes. While waiting, I packed a bag with essentials in case Max's hospital stay lasted longer than expected. My mind was racing with millions of thoughts. But I forced myself not to panic. Maybe it was stress. Maybe exhaustion. That's how I justified it to myself. Max had never been sick. He was strong, healthy, an athlete who took care of himself. It couldn't be anything serious. When Matilda arrived, I nearly broke my nose running into the doorframe as I rushed to let her in. I handed Adam to her, kissing him hard on the forehead. I barely managed a full sentence before bolting toward the garage.

The hospital was close. But the drive felt like hours. I hit every red light. I was shaking. When I finally arrived, I practically threw my car into the first available parking space and sprinted inside. I ran straight to the reception desk, where a middle-aged nurse—or maybe a receptionist, I had no idea—stood waiting. I didn't even bother with pleasantries. "Max Frans?" I gasped, my voice shaky and loud. She pointed down a long hallway. I ran. Above the entrance, a sign read: Oncology. I checked every room. I must have passed half the ward before

I finally found him. Max was sitting up in a hospital bed. He looked exactly the same as when they took him away. It had only been an hour since I last saw him. He seemed… fine. I had worried for nothing.

I flew into the room, threw myself at him, wrapping my arms around his neck. I didn't want to ever let go. Tears flooded my face—again. I had been so scared. "Baby, I'm here now. I'm so sorry I couldn't come with you." I kissed his forehead, then his lips. "Alice, I'm fine," he reassured me. "I'm a grown man. You had to stay with Adam, I understand. Don't worry anymore. I'm okay. You're here now. I'm sorry I scared you like that." "I was terrified," I admitted. From now on, I'll be making all the meals! You are banned from the kitchen! We both laughed. But then—

A voice interrupted us. "Good morning, Mr. Frans. I'm Dr. Turban." A middle-aged man stood at the door. "Good morning," Max replied. I cut him off. "Alice. Max's fiancée. What's wrong with him? Why was he brought to oncology?" Max tried to brush it off. "Alice, I just fainted from exhaustion. That's all." But the doctor's expression changed. "I'm afraid it's more than that. Mr. Frans, we suspect it's cancer. Thyroid cancer." The doctor continued explaining the next steps, but for me, it was already too much. My gaze fixed on one of the wheels of the hospital bed beside me. I had no idea how long I sat there like that, but I couldn't hear anything else. This had to be a mistake. "Please, test my fiancé again. And then test him again. This isn't possible. Max is strong. He's healthy. This cannot be true!" I interrupted the conversation between the doctor and Max, my voice rising with desperation. It wasn't real. It couldn't be real.

Only then did I realize I was still sitting—where Max had gently placed me himself. He had positioned me there with his hands, as if he was the one comforting me. His palm rested on my knee, his fingers softly tracing small circles on my skin. "Miss, I assure you, we will conduct all the necessary tests. But this is the most probable diagnosis," the doctor said, his voice calm yet heavy. For now, Mr. Frans will need to stay in the hospital. He sighed. "I'm very sorry." And with that, he disappeared beyond the hospital room doorway. I hadn't even had time to feel relieved that Max was okay. And now? I broke down again, tears flooding my face. What now?

I lay on the hospital bed, unable to sleep. The clock was nearing 5:00 a.m., and my mind was racing with a thousand thoughts.How could I have fallen in love with a woman I might have to leave all alone? I can't die.

We have our whole lives ahead of us. If the test results come back bad, what am I supposed to do? Thinking about that only brings one person to my mind—Alice. Her face. Her reaction when she heard the news. I was supposed to protect her, take care of her—not the other way around. I wanted to be her superhero forever. Instead, it might turn out the other way around. I don't know if I could ever let her watch me suffer. If I had to go, it would break my heart. But hers would break first.

I didn't want to sink into dark thoughts, so I thought of her instead. Her smile. The way she pouts when she's annoyed. Sometimes I feel like I can't even express how much I love her. Our life runs its course like any other, but I regret not being a millionaire, not spending every second with her— whether in bed, on vacations, or just curled up in our living room arm-chairs. I can't imagine life without my best friend. She's the one person I can tell everything to. It's almost funny. We can laugh for hours over the dumbest things, and then... We somehow end up in bed or in the bathtub, acting like a couple who should probably be filming a porno.

This woman ignites every part of my soul—With her body, her words, and even her smallest gestures. She's the one. And the best part? She loves me the same way. That's true hap-piness— knowing you are someone's whole world. And I know that. Every time she wakes up, her eyes say, "Hey, Max... you're my everything." Just thinking about it makes tears well up in my eyes. I can't let her down. I can't leave her. I must live. For her. For Adam.

I'm a father, a partner, a husband-to-be. I want to wake up next to her for the next 30 years. To chase after our kids. To argue over stupid little things. To keep my hand on her knee during every road trip. This has to happen. I'm not going anywhere. Pull yourself together, Max. The clock reads 7:00 a.m. I haven't slept all night, but I feel strong. The doctor said he would be here with my results this morning. I just hope Alice doesn't arrive before him. I don't want her to go through yesterday's pain again. I hate seeing tears on her face. I worry about how she's really handling this. What did she do when she got home? I called her last night. She lied. She told me everything was fine. She lied to me for the first time in her life. I know she only did it so I wouldn't worry.

"Good morning, Mr. Frans. How did you sleep?" The doctor entered my hospital room "Great, doctor." I didn't want to admit to my sleepless night. I have your results. I took a deep breath. Here's the situation: You have thyroid cancer. We need to completely remove your thyroid, as well as the nearby lymph nodes. Hopefully, everything will go as planned. I nodded, forcing myself to stay calm. "I understand. But... can you tell me more? I need to know. "
The doctor sighed. "For now, things look promising. We don't see any metastasis. However, during the operation, anything can happen. But... we are optimistic." "Thank you. When is the surgery? What do I need to do?" "For now, just rest. Today, you can go home. You'll receive your scheduled surgery date when you're discharged. Goodbye, Mr. Frans." And with that, he left.

At 8:00 a.m. sharp, Alice arrived. She told me she had been waiting since 7:30. Of course, she had. I asked her about Adam—I missed him so much. I asked about Matilda—if her job was giving her trouble for taking time off. And I asked about her. How she was feeling. "Max, I'm fine." She lied again. I know those eyes. She cried all night. I reached for her hand and pulled her into my lap. "Baby, I'm going to be okay. The doctor came by earlier." "What did he say? What happens next? Max, I'm so worried." She leaned her forehead against mine, running her fingers through my hair. "I have thyroid cancer. I need surgery to remove my thyroid and lymph nodes. The doctor believes it will go well." She took a deep breath. Max... "I need to tell you something. " I raised an eyebrow. "I'm listening, love. But... if it's bad news, say it now. If it's something beautiful, wait until we get home. I don't want to have a special moment in a damn hospital." She smiled softly. "Okay. Let's go home. We'll talk there." She kissed my nose.

Alice stepped outside for a moment, telling me to gather my things. I noticed her making a phone call, but I didn't have time to ask who it was. I packed my bag as fast as I could. I just wanted to go home. I couldn't wait to hold Adam in my arms. To drink morning coffee by the fireplace. To spend the night with my beautiful fiancée. I felt good. I just wanted to live our life. I didn't need anything else.

As I walked out of the hospital, I received my discharge documents along with the date for my surgery—two weeks from now. Two weeks of waiting. Two weeks of doubt. Two weeks of torment. I wasn't thrilled about how long I'd have to wait, but there was nothing I could do about it. The moment we crossed the hospital threshold, Alice banned me from driving until I felt better and ordered me to take a leave from work. She was right. Whether I liked it or not, I needed to stay home and rest. I decided not to argue with her.

On the drive back, she filled the silence with stories about what she and Adam had been up to. She talked about her chores. The vinyl records she had played from my collection. And finally, she admitted to a sleepless night and buckets of tears. Yet, today, her face looked brighter. I had no idea why. I could only hope that it was my return that lifted her spirits. There was nothing more beautiful in the world than

Alice's smile. Sick or healthy, I would always laugh with her. We pulled into the driveway, gathering my things from the car. Alice, caught in a frenzy, kept snatching everything from my hands. I understood she was worried, but I was her man— I was going to be fine. I felt strong. I would get through this.

I noticed a crowd of at least six neighbors watching us from across the street as Alice struggled to lift my suitcase from the trunk. Considering she was a full foot shorter and at least fifty pounds lighter than me, I was sure the spectacle looked ridiculous. Of course, we burst into laughter until our neighbors finally turned away and went back inside. I had only been gone a day and a half, but I felt like I had been away for half a life-time. I had missed our home. I had missed the smell of it. I had missed our bedroom. Adam's toys scattered everywhere. And her— The way she walked around in just her underwear. The way she hung laundry on the clothesline outside. The way she made us feel like a family. I had missed it all so much.

Crossing the threshold, something felt off. Something wasn't right. The keys that were usually tossed on the cabinets were gone. The light in the living room was different—warmer. Did Alice throw a party? No, that didn't seem right. Stepping into the living room, I was met with a breathtaking sight— Thousands of candles. They were everywhere. A wine bottle and a single large glass sat on the coffee table. The entire house was lit only by the flickering flames. And on the table, next to a rosary, was a small, rectangular box. "Welcome home, love!" Alice's voice rang out as she hugged me from behind, pressing a soft kiss to my neck. "Baby, I was only gone for a day…" We both laughed.

Alice kicked off her black-and-gold heels, settling grace-fully into one of our armchairs. I followed, sinking into the chair beside her. I couldn't help myself. Just like in the beginning. I slid from my seat to my knees, slowly making my way toward her chair. I gently parted her legs, pressing soft kisses against her thighs. "Max… first, sit down and open your present." She stopped me, cupping my face with one hand while brushing a stray lock of hair from my forehead with the other. I reluctantly returned to my seat, reaching for the small gift box wrapped in white decorative paper.

I had no clue what it could be. Maybe a pen. Or a fancy spoon. But when I opened it, my heart stopped. Inside was a plastic test stick— A pregnancy test. And on the front, in bold letters: Positive. Alice's voice was soft but steady. "Max, I'm pregnant. You're going to be a father." My legs buckled. I fell to my knees, forehead pressed against the floor. And then I broke down completely. I sobbed so loudly I was sure I had woken up the entire neighborhood. They were probably already filing noise complaints.

I cried, rubbed my eyes, ran my hands through my hair. Alice dropped down beside me, pulling my head to her chest. Her hands were gentle as she wiped my tears. "Max, are you okay?" She kissed my forehead. "Alice... baby... I... " I struggled for words. The only thing that came out was— "I love you so much, baby." I pulled her into my arms as tightly as I could. She had already become everything in my life. And now, she was about to become the mother of our child. My dream. Our dream. A family.

We spent the evening curled up by the fireplace, her hands in mine. She settled onto my lap, looking into my eyes while running her fingers through my hair. "Where's Adam?" I asked. "With Matilda." "For the whole night?" She grinned. "For the whole night."

That night was unlike any other. We made love everywhere. On the kitchen counter. On the armchairs. Against the living room wall. In the hallway. On the stairs. God knows where else— Until we finally collapsed into bed. I didn't know where all this energy came from. Maybe it was love. Or longing. Or the sheer joy of knowing our family was growing. After hours of giving in to each other, we finally talked. Alice told me how she suspected she was pregnant. And I— I was still trying to figure out when it happened. We were intimate nearly every other night, and it never got old. We were so happy we almost forgot about my illness.

"Max, you're going to be a father. You can't leave us," Alice began. "I don't know if you'll understand what I'm about to say, but I would die without you. You are everything to me." "Baby, I'm not going anywhere. Especially not now. We have so much to do— the wedding, preparing the nursery, transferring the house to your name, and…" Alice cut me off. Why would you transfer the house to us?" she asked, sitting up naked in our bed, covering herself with the edge of the blanket. ""Why do you want to do this?" "No. I want to put everything in your name. Not just the house. Everything. Today everything is fine, but if something were to happen to me… " Before I could finish, she threw on her white robe and left the bedroom without a word.

I lay there in our bed for a while, knowing exactly why she reacted this way. But I had to tell her. I knew everything would turn out the way we wanted, but I needed to protect her. To protect them— Alice, Adam, and our unborn child. I didn't want to hurt her, but she had to understand me. If she were in my position, she would do the same. I couldn't protect them any other way— Not if I wasn't there. I lasted about half an hour alone. It felt like torture. Running a hand through my hair, I got up and headed to the kitchen, where I could hear Alice. As I stepped inside, I saw my future wife leaning against the counter. The look on her face—I had never seen her this angry before. I had thrown her completely off balance. I knew exactly why she felt this way. She refused to accept the possibility of losing me, so she didn't want me to transfer everything to her. As if not doing it would somehow keep me alive. But of course, that's not how it works. I needed to explain.

"Baby, why did you leave?" I asked gently. "This was supposed to be our night. Just tell me— what's on your mind?" She tapped her fingers against the counter, her lips pressing into a firm line. "Max, I'm angry. Because you've already accepted that you're going to leave us. And I don't want you to do that. Please... fight for all of this. I believe that after the surgery, everything will be fine." "Baby, I believe that too. No one said I'm doing this because I think I'm going to die. I've always wanted to do this. Whether today or tomorrow. Whether I'm healthy or not." "I don't want to talk about this anymore. Do what you want. I trust you. But my anger isn't going away anytime soon." She crossed her arms over her chest, glaring at me.

I sighed, taking a step closer. "Alright. We'll do it this way — I'll transfer everything to you... after the surgery. Does that sound better?" I paused, waiting for her reaction. "Either way, I'm going to do it. But this way, you'll know that I'm not doing it just because of my illness. It's a compromise." Alice narrowed her eyes at me for a moment. Then she exhaled sharply. "Fine. But you're still sleeping in bed tonight," she huffed, turning toward the hallway. "And if you change anything in our deal — you'll be sleeping in the chair by the fireplace!" She shot me at one last pointed look before disappearing into our bedroom.

Our days were so full of energy and activities that I completely lost track of what day of the week it was. We were constantly on the move — attending different medical appointments that Alice found online, researching yoga, and shopping for our little one. I had never seen clothes, shoes, or diapers so tiny in my life. Every time we came across something cute in a store, Alice would check the price, and I'd shoot her a look that said, "Come on, don't worry about it!" After visiting a few stores, she gave up trying to be frugal, and we simply bought whatever was needed and adorable, without looking at the cost.

We still didn't know our baby's gender — it was only the second month of pregnancy, so there was plenty of time to find out. But for me, it didn't matter, and I knew Alice felt the same way. I couldn't wait for the day our child would arrive. I thought about it constantly. That day would make me even happier, and Alice wouldn't just be the love of my life, she'd also become the mother of my child. Every morning, I asked her how she was feeling, whether she had any nausea or cravings for something special. I knew it was still early in the pregnancy, but so far, Alice was surprisingly normal—that's the best way I could describe it. We still made love just as passionately as always. Her appetite and behavior remained the same as before. And then, the time finally came. I packed the essentials in my bag and dressed in comfortable clothes, which seemed like the right choice for surgery day. I had never experienced anything like this before. I had no idea what to bring or if I even needed to bring anything at all. Alice didn't sleep all night. She kept waking up, either crying or going to the kitchen for a glass of water. My heart broke for her. I didn't know how to help. No one had ever worried about me this much before. It was a strange, beautiful, and terrifying feeling all at once. I couldn't forgive myself for putting her through this. And in her condition, she shouldn't be dealing with so much stress.

I did everything I could in the days leading up to the surgery. I distracted her with baby-related tasks, took Alice and Adam to the playground more often, and even stuffed our candy drawer so full of treats that it barely closed. I was doing everything I could—But so was she. Every meal she cooked for me in those final days felt like it came from a five-star restaurant. She took care of me and never left my side. Even our sex life became more passionate than ever before. She even introduced new things in bed, completely surprising me— And I was in seventh heaven.

She wanted to make me feel so good that she truly helped me forget that in just a few days, complete strangers—people who didn't care about me the way she did—would be cutting into my body. On our way to the hospital, we dropped Adam off at Matilda's house. He was thrilled to be there, and she was just as happy to take care of him. I was grateful that Alice had such a close friend. But I also felt sorry for Matilda— She was an amazing woman, yet life seemed to make things so difficult for her. She had bad luck with men and so many other things. I even considered setting her up on a blind date, but she told me she'd only think about it once everything calmed down with us. Alice had told me that she hadn't fully appreciated their friendship before— Not until both had faced hardships. Only then did they truly understand each other. I was glad she had a Matilda. She was a good person— She reminded me of my sister. Kind. Caring. But also, someone who could spice up a conversation when needed. She was an interesting person.

During the entire drive to the hospital, Alice and I held hands or touched in some way. I don't know why, but I absolutely loved it when she ran her fingers through my hair. She always did it so gently and sensually— Every time, it sent a rush of heat through my body. And she knew it. She always knew how much I liked it. But I could feel how nervous she was. She spoke quickly, swallowing hard between sentences. I tried to calm her down, but nothing helped. The more I tried, the more upset she became.

I didn't want this to be my last day. All night, I kept telling myself: "Max! It's just thyroid cancer! They'll remove what they need to, and that's it!" At first, I was terrified. But now, I was confident— That's exactly how it would go. We stepped through the hospital doors and entered the ward where I was scheduled. The nurses handed me a hospital gown and a set of towels. Alice never let go of my hand. I felt relieved that the day had finally come— But also scared. Not for myself. For her. If something happened to me, I wouldn't be afraid of dying. I was afraid of never being able to kiss the love of my life again. Of never seeing Adam's smile again. Of never meeting our child. The doctor assured me that everything would be fine, But fear whispered in the back of my mind— This isn't just a cold. I had called my specialist several times, asking how I should prepare and what to expect. I learned that after surgery, my voice might change, my wound might bleed, and I could develop hoarseness— Which might go away after a few days... Or it might not. I would have to limit physical activity—Which meant even our sex life would be affected. I might also develop hypothyroidism. I knew everything I needed to know. Now, I just had to undergo surgery— And then live the rest of my life beside the most wonderful woman in the world.

Two nurses led me toward the operating room. They offered me a wheelchair. Maybe it would've been fun. But I refused. I couldn't bear the thought of Alice pushing me when I was supposed to be the one protecting her. She never left my side. I was so lucky to have her—But also ashamed of what I was putting her through. It felt awful. I missed her smile more than anything. I had been pretending that everything was fine— But the truth was, nothing was normal. I never imagined that the love of my life would be the one holding my hand as I was wheeled into an operating room. This was it. The next step.

"Baby, everything will be fine. Please, don't worry," I told her, looking into her eyes. "I love you. I'll be back soon. You and Adam are everything. I promise—I'll come back to you." Alice kissed every one of my fingers, holding my hands between hers. "Max, we're waiting for you. I love you. Just come back." She ran her fingers through my hair, tucking it behind my ears, and whispered: "I'll be right here. I love you. I'll see you soon." I turned my head— And let my tears fall.

I waited in the hospital corridor for about three hours. So many people passed by— Elderly women clutching handkerchiefs, and younger people anxiously glancing at the clock hanging above the operating room doors. I felt like I couldn't handle waiting any longer— Until suddenly, Max's doctor appeared. Ms. Frans? he asked. I had no energy to explain that I wasn't officially Max's wife yet. "Yes, that's me. Good morning," I replied. The surgery is over. I'm not sure when he will wake up…" I cut him off before he could say more. "How is he? Is he okay?" I asked quickly. "I believe the procedure went well," the doctor explained. "There will be post-operative complications, of course. Regular monitoring will be necessary, but as of today, I am optimistic." "Thank you," I whispered. I had no strength to say anything more.

When they finally allowed me to enter Max's hospital room several hours later, I felt like I was in heaven— Just because I could see him again. His face was so pale— He lay on the bed as if he were completely exhausted But still, he was my Max. Nothing in my life had ever brought me more relief than just seeing his face. Suddenly, I felt my phone vibrate. But there was nothing more important than being here with him, So I didn't even look at it. Adam was safe with Matilda. Our baby was growing inside me. And I was holding Max's hand. Nothing else mattered. But then, my phone vibrated again.

After a moment, I finally decided to check it. I saw a missed call from Matilda— And a message "Alice, I know nothing is more important right now, but I must tell you this. Olaf is back. A policeman—one who knows Max—called me. Apparently, Olaf returned to his old place. His friends say he's worse than before. Please be careful. Adam is asleep. Don't worry. – Matilda" As I read her message, I felt a horrible wave of anxiety crash over me. I already had enough problems. I didn't need more. I held Max's hand for nearly two hours. I thought about our future. And I realized— Now I had to be the one to take care of us. I had no strength left for more worries.

When Max wakes up, the first thing I tell him won't be that Olaf is back. Max is exhausted—He just had surgery. I don't want to stress him out even more. Suddenly, I felt his hand squeeze mine. He started to move slightly. I quickly looked up and kissed his hand again. "Baby?" Max's voice was hoarse, his eyes still closed. "Yes, it's me. I'm here," I whispered. "I love you so much… tell me quickly. Is everything okay?" he asked weakly. "I love you too. I'm right here. Don't worry. Everything is fine. Just rest". I didn't want him to hear the worry in my voice. "What did the doctor say?" Max continued. "He said the surgery went well, and you're okay. There will be complications, but you're going to be fine," I explained.

I noticed a tear rolling down his cheek. In his eyes, I saw both calmness and fear. He was afraid—And I didn't blame him. The only thing I could do was be by his side— Support him. Take care of him. And that's exactly what I intended to do. The man of my life needed me. And I would be right here— Always.

Chapter 12

A Strand That Held

After two days, I was finally able to bring Max home. We were both overjoyed. We had had enough of those gloomy hospital corridors. All we wanted was to sit in our armchairs, talk about everything and nothing, and simply enjoy being together. Max looked good, but I noticed some changes. His voice was much hoarser, he occasionally complained about pain near the surgical wound, and he even had a fever twice. We didn't panic—the doctor had already told us about all the possible post-operative complications. We were prepared, we just had to stay strong. Everything was going to be okay.

Throughout the car ride home, Max kept his hand on my thigh. I trembled the entire time. I wanted him to touch me, but I also knew that if he didn't stop, he wouldn't be getting any rest at home. We hadn't been intimate for a week, and I knew Max would want our first night back together to be in bed. But he needed rest. I already had a speech planned in my head—to refuse him. I knew he'd pretended nothing hurt, that he wasn't tired, and he'd push through the exhaustion just to be with me. That's who he was. As Max stepped over the threshold of our home, he insisted on carrying his own bag—claiming he was fine. I followed him inside. Matilda was already there, holding Adam in her arms. "Good morning, little angel!" Max exclaimed, his voice stronger as he rushed over to Adam, kissing his forehead before snatching him from Matilda's arms. "I missed you so much," he added, hugging Adam in the sweetest way imaginable. Matilda smiled.

"Alright, I'm heading out. If you need anything, just call me. We'll stay in touch. Oh! And Max! She pointed a finger at him. Take it easy! Spending one night alone won't kill you!" Max just grinned. "I'm so glad this is finally over," Matilda said softly, kissing his cheek before heading for the door. "Bye, love-birds!" she called out, closing the front door behind her. Max turned to me with Adam still in his arms. "So, it's just us now. You, me, and our children," he said with a warm smile, hugging Adam closer to his chest.

The entire day was spent playing with Adam. At one point, we laughed so hard our stomachs hurt. I was so happy— we were together as a family, just the three of us. I didn't need anything else. The love of my life was home, my son was with us, and our baby was growing safely inside me. "I'll put Adam to bed tonight. You go rest, take a bath, I'll come to you," Max said, picking Adam up. Wait for me. "Max, shouldn't you be the one resting?" I asked, raising an eyebrow. "Maybe I should wait for you in the bathroom?" I teased. "That's a fantastic idea. We'll relax together. And besides," he smirked, "we have a few things to discuss."

He kissed my forehead before disappearing into the bedroom with Adam. I headed to our bathroom, grabbing my favorite robe and some fresh towels on the way. I pulled the curtains shut and filled the bathtub with warm water. I was just about to undress when— Max walked in. He was smiling. His color had returned—He looked better. Nothing was better for his health than being at home with us. Max set up the baby monitor on the counter before walking toward me. He closed the distance between us until there were only inches between our faces. One hand cupped my cheek, while the other loosened the belt of my robe— Then, he placed his palm on my hip and pulled me close. I knew exactly what he wanted— I knew him too well. I didn't want him to strain himself tonight. Or... maybe I did—But I also knew he needed rest. Then again, he was a grown man—He knew his own limits.

Before I could finish that thought, I felt my robe and his clothes hit the floor. A gentle touch caressed my thighs and moved between my legs. And then, in the blink of an eye, I was in his arms. One arm supported my back, The other held me firmly by my waist. My legs wrapped around him as he pressed me against his body. "I love you I missed you so much," Max whispered. I didn't get the chance to respond. Because the next thing I knew— We were making love right there, In the middle of our bathroom.

I had no idea that after just a week without sex, I would start losing my mind. From the moment we got into the car, all I could think about was Alice's naked body and how this day was going to end. I knew I should have been resting, but I couldn't help myself. Holding Alice in my arms, standing in the middle of our bathroom, I felt like the most refreshed man on Earth. This was exactly what I needed, what I had missed. Her touch, her taste, her scent. I was grateful that the worst was behind us, and I would be able to experience this with her for the rest of my life. We had eternity ahead of us. Our love-making that night was incredible. We were so passionate that we both kept glancing nervously at the baby monitor— We didn't want to wake Adam. But we missed each other too much—physically and emotionally. There was no other way for this day to end. We explored each other in every possible way, in every possible place. I was impressed. Sex with Alice had always been amazing, but this separation had somehow made it even more intense. I covered every inch of her body with kisses—I was inside her so many times that I felt strange whenever I wasn't. Her moans, her whispers, drove me to madness. I gave her everything I had, and she did the same for me. No one in my entire life had ever made me feel more satisfied in bed than her. And the best part? She was mine. My fiancée. Soon to be my wife. I had no idea what I had done to deserve her. I was the luckiest man alive.

When our love marathon was over, we soaked in a bath full of bubbles. We stayed in the water so long that our fingers wrinkled, and our lips turned blue. After we finally got out, we brushed our teeth together and wrapped ourselves in our matching white robes. Then, we headed to the kitchen. Alice sat down in her favorite chair, and I lit the fireplace. Tell me, love… what's bothering you? I asked as I sat beside her. I felt that Alice was hiding something. I knew you'd notice, she sighed. I need to tell you something. I wanted to wait as long as possible… because of your condition. If I survived tonight, I could handle anything, I smirked. But Alice's face darkened. Olaf is back. Apparently, he's worse than before, she said, lowering her head. My hands immediately clenched into fists. What? When did he come back? Today? I demanded. A few days ago, she admitted. I… I didn't want to worry you. Olaf—the man who tried to hurt you—came back, and you didn't tell me? Are you insane? How could you? I could feel my anger rising. My face turned red, and I couldn't sit still. I got up and walked into the kitchen, pouring myself a glass of water to calm down. I'm sorry, Max… Alice whispered. I didn't want to continue this conversation. I was angry—but more than that, I was disappointed. It was my job to protect my family. How could no one tell me sooner? I grabbed my phone and called a friend in the police force. He told me everything I should have known from the start. Olaf was back. He knew where Alice lived. He knew which preschool Adam attended. He knew where she worked. He even knew that she was pregnant and that we were planning to get married. He knew everything. What was I supposed to do? I couldn't lock myself and my family inside the house forever. I had to be a man—I had to handle this. Besides, nothing had happened yet. Maybe he had finally given up? Maybe he moved on? I would have been a fool to believe that. Two months have passed since my surgery. I started working from home—I didn't want to waste my leave because I knew I'd need it when our baby was born. Alice continued her regular check-ups, taking great care of herself. She was happy, truly glowing. I noticed changes in her body. Her breasts were fuller, her stomach was rounder. She looked beautiful—even more than before.

Every morning, I kissed her belly, right above her navel— That's where I could feel our little girl the most. We took care of each other—She watched over my health, and I took care of her. Our baby was growing perfectly, and in just four months, she would be here. I was so happy that I woke up every morning wondering if this was all just a dream. After our last doctor's visit, we finally found out— Our baby was a girl. She was healthy and growing beautifully. When I saw the first clear ultrasound photo of her, I couldn't hold back my tears. I had seen her on the screen many times before— But this time, I truly saw her. Her face, her tiny hands and feet. She was real. Alice and I had created something so perfect. I still couldn't believe it. On the car ride home, Alice was deep in thought. I knew she was thinking about telling me the name she had chosen. I gave her time. "Lidia," she finally said. "I want to name our daughter Lidia." She turned to me and smiled. "It's beautiful," I replied, kissing her hand. I had never been picky about names. But Lidia—it was perfect. The days flew by.

One morning, while having breakfast, I got a silent phone call. Alice's phone rang right after mine—Another silent call. We got four more of those mysterious calls that day. The odds of someone accidentally dialing both of us were too small to ignore. Later that afternoon, we went shopping for baby supplies and spent time at the park with Adam. Everything felt perfect— until I walked to a nearby shop to grab some water. For some reason, I had a strange feeling. Like something bad was about to happen. Fifteen minutes later, I returned— And Alice was gone.

Sitting on the park bench, waiting for Max, I suddenly heard someone calling my name. I immediately turned around — And there he was. Drunk. Olaf. I was so shocked that I instantly jumped to my feet, my mind calculating how far I was from Adam, who was playing in the sandbox. "Well, hello there. Aren't you gonna greet me? I bet you missed me!" Olaf shouted, his voice slurring as he staggered toward me. I froze. Instinctively, my hand flew to my stomach, as if I could shield my unborn child just from his words alone. Slowly, I began stepping backward, inching toward Adam. But Olaf mirrored my movements, closing the distance. He was now less than five steps away. My heart pounded in my chest. I was terrified. "Don't come any closer, Olaf, or I'll call the police!" I warned, my voice shaking as I continued toward Adam.

Suddenly, Olaf was only two meters away. "I missed you both. I know everything about you, Alice. You can never hide from me—understand? I could've forgiven you for being a whore, but getting yourself knocked up? You're just a pathetic slut. Did that sick idiot brainwash Adam too?" He laughed, stepping even closer. "Olaf, I'm warning you," I raised my voice, desperately hoping someone—anyone—would step in. But I knew I wouldn't win against him. He was right in front of me now— Face to face. "I just want to hug my son, and you— You should come back to me. No one will ever treat you as well as I did. Remember our passionate nights?" His hands grabbed at me. I fought him off with all my strength.

"Remember our future plans? The birth of Max?" Olaf's voice was mocking, his hands roaming where they weren't wanted. "Yes, I remember! I remember how you raped me at night! I remember how you showed up drunk after I gave birth, just to see Adam! You're a monster!" I screamed the words right into his face.

There were only three children left playing on the playground—and just two parents. I had hoped someone would step in. But instead, I saw them picking up their kids and walking away. I didn't blame them. I would have done the same. "What did you just say to me?" Olaf's voice darkened. Then—A sudden impact. A fall. And the piercing scream of Adam. Maybe it's better that I don't remember the rest of that afternoon.

I couldn't believe my own eyes. It is Olaf. Where the hell did, he come from? I was still a few meters away from the playground when I saw him. And then—He grabbed Alice. At first, he shoved her several times by the shoulders. Then—He punched her. Twice. Hard. Right in the stomach. Like she was just a sack of potatoes. I screamed his name, my voice roaring through the air. My legs burned as I sprinted toward them, pulling out my phone with one hand. I pressed speed dial—number two. I had arranged this long ago with my friend on the force. Instantly, he received our location. And, he knew something was wrong.

I reached Alice and dropped to my knees, trying to help her up. But I hesitated. If Olaf had seriously hurt her, moving her might make it worse. That's when I saw it—The red stains spreading across her beige dress. Blood. My mind shattered. What the hell do I do first? Help Alice? Run to Adam? Kill Olaf with my bare hands? As I knelt beside Alice, I heard her whisper. "Max... Adam…" That's when it hit me. Adam. I turned my head and saw Olaf. He was kneeling in the sand, speaking to Adam. "Get away from him, you psychopath!" I roared, my voice shaking the air. "Oh, look. The prince on a white horse. The hero. Adam is my son, and I'm taking him home."

Olaf reached out his hands to Adam. To his shock, Adam backed away. With tears in his eyes, my boy sprinted toward me. Olaf lunged to grab him, cursing, shouting awful insults. But he failed. Adam leaped into my arms—And I positioned myself to shield both him and Alice. Then, I saw it. Olaf reached behind his back. He pulled out a gun. A gun. Where the hell did he get it? How did he afford it? My stomach turned to ice. "Give me my son." Olaf aimed the barrel right at me. Suddenly, Alice lifted herself up. Tears streaming down her face, she screamed. "Leave them alone, you bastard! Leave them!" She looked terrifying, more furious than I had ever seen her before. "You hurt me, Alice. Now I'm going to hurt you." "Please, Olaf. I'm begging you. Don't do this." Alice's voice broke into a sob. Then, finally, the sound of sirens. A police car. Olaf smirked. "You're not my baby girl anymore." And then he pulled the trigger.

The gun fired straight at me and Adam. I knew that I had no other choice and, even if I did, I would've done the same. I clutched Adam tightly in my arms and spun my body around. The bullet hit me. Somewhere near my stomach. I looked down at Adam. It all happened in seconds, but I had enough time to register that he wasn't hurt. I collapsed to my knees. Then to my side. Adam didn't leave me. Not for a second. He laid beside me in silence, his small hands pressing against my neck. I crawled toward Alice—And covered her with my body. I was terrified that Olaf would shoot again. Then, more gunfire. I held Adam even closer, shielding Alice as much as I could.

Then I heard it—the voice of my friend from the police. "CALL ANOTHER AMBULANCE! Jesus Christ, there's blood everywhere!" I turned my head. Olaf was lying in a pool of blood. He'd been shot. Maybe he was dead. Maybe he wasn't. But I felt a wave of relief. And at the same time—Fear. What the hell just happened? Would Alice and our baby be, okay? How would this affect Adam? Then, a small voice." Daddy?" The sweetest thing I could have ever heard. For the first time— Adam called me Dad. Despite everything—It made my heart swell. I was his father. And I loved him as my own son. I would give my life for him. And for Alice. I kissed Adam's forehead and whispered, "It's okay, sweetheart. It's over."

I turned to Alice. She was covered in blood, her face pale, her hands shaking. She looked like she was about to lose consciousness. "Baby, hold on. The ambulance is coming. I love you. Everything will be okay." I kissed her face again and again, as if it could somehow fix everything. But the truth was—I had no idea if anything would be okay. I lay there for what felt like twenty minutes. Maybe longer. Alice could barely blink. But she was holding on. Adam stood beside me, clutching my hand. I had only one job left—stay awake. But my body gave in. I lost consciousness, still holding Alice's and Adam's hands.

When I woke up, I was in the hospital, a bandage wrapped around my stomach. I felt weak, but stable. Sitting beside me was my sister. "Where's Alice? What about the baby? Where's Adam?" "Max, calm down. You need to rest." "TELL ME!" She sighed. "Alice is in another room. She lost a lot of blood. She passed out. We don't know anything yet. "I need to see her. " I tried to get up. "Max, you're not going anywhere." "Where did I get hit?" "You took a bullet to the stomach. You lost a lot of blood, but nothing major was damaged. You'll survive." Then she added, "You'll probably need rehabilitation." I stared at her. She was hiding something. I could feel it.

I could feel the anger she had towards my fiancée, but I wasn't entirely sure why. She had never liked Alice—I knew that. She was always worried about me, afraid that being with Alice would get me hurt. And this time, she was right. But regardless of what happened, she knew that nothing would change my mind. I was going to be with Alice whether she liked it or not. She often seemed to forget that Alice was carrying my child, that we were planning our wedding and a future together. I was also determined to adopt Adam—I saw it as a necessity. I wanted us to be a family.

"What about him?" I threw the question toward my sister. "Alice's ex?" she asked. "Believe it or not, they locked him up, but apparently, he has a good lawyer. They're saying there's a chance he might get released. I'm sorry, Max. They claim he was under the influence of drugs or had lost consciousness at the time," she explained. I had no words. I couldn't even begin to comprehend the idea that Olaf might still be out there, walking around like a normal person, living his life after what he had done.

I started pulling on my clothes. I couldn't sit still any longer. "Max, did you hear what I just said? You're not going anywhere!" This time, she raised her voice, but I'd had enough. "For fuck's sake! I'm getting dressed, and I'm going to check on Alice and my child. If you think you can stop me, you're dead wrong. Stop trying to hold me back! Just give me some damn peace!" I snapped, marching toward her. My sister left the room but returned moments later with a wheelchair. I guess she finally realized she wasn't going to stop me.

I headed toward the room where Alice was staying. From what I had learned, Matilda had taken Adam home. He was safe, though in shock. Thankfully, he was now in good hands. Matilda loved that little boy as much as we did, and I knew he was protected. My sister pushed my wheelchair while I searched for Alice with my eyes. We passed dozens of doors, behind which women were recovering from childbirth or still carrying their unborn children. I had no idea what was happening with Alice, and the mere thought sent shivers down my spine. We finally reached one of the last rooms—I found her.

My sister wheeled me right up to the bedside and left the room, resting a reassuring hand on my shoulder before she exited. It was her silent way of supporting me. Alice was hooked up to multiple IVs. She looked terrible, I had never seen her like this. The moment I saw her; I broke down in tears. I cried like a child. I wasn't even sure if it was out of relief that I could see her or out of anguish that she had ended up here and that I had failed to protect her. I took her hand in mine and pressed it onto my face. My tears were falling so heavily that they left wet marks on the white sheets covering her bed. I couldn't stop myself. "Max…" Alice whispered in a hoarse, barely audible voice. "Are you okay?"

" My love, I'll be fine, don't worry. But what about you? I don't know anything. I love you, sweetheart. I'm so, so sorry," I said, kissing her hand even harder. "Where is she?" Alice asked. "Who, darling?" I asked, confused. "Max… our baby," she said, and my heart nearly stopped. "What about her?" I pressed further, fear gripping me. Alice was too weak to keep answering my questions. From the way she spoke, I could tell something was wrong with our baby. I had to find out. I glanced at Alice's belly—it looked slightly smaller.

A wave of terror crashed over me. I didn't want to leave her, but if she had the strength to speak, she would have told me to go check on our child. And so, that's what I did. I called my sister, and we rushed to the room where several doctors were gathered. I knocked on the door and asked about Alice. "Good morning. Max Frans, I'm here about—" One of the doctors didn't let me finish. "Ah, good morning, Mr. Frans. You're Ms. Alice's fiancé, correct? What a terrible tragedy. My deepest sympathies," the doctor said. I tensed immediately, not knowing if he was referring to the events of yesterday or if something had happened to our unborn daughter. The doctor stepped out into the hallway with me. "Mr. Frans," he said, placing a firm hand on my shoulder. Ms. Alice is in bad shape but stable. The blow to her stomach was severe, and she lost a significant amount of blood. We had to perform surgery. Her condition is critical, but she is stable, she will recover," he explained. Tears welled up in my eyes again. This time, I buried my face in my hands, overwhelmed by emotions. "And what about the baby?" I managed to ask, trying to keep my voice steady.

"We had to perform an emergency C-section. Your daughter is in the care of our specialists. She's in an incubator. Personally, I believe she's strong—just like her mother—and she's going to be okay," the doctor said. At that, I completely lost control. I didn't know whether I was crying out of happiness or because of the weight of everything that had just happened. "What? Where is she? Please, take me to her," I begged.

I had just learned that I had become a father. Never in my life would I have imagined that it would happen under such horrific circumstances. I had read a lot about childbirth, pregnancy, and everything in between. I had wanted to be prepared. I knew that babies could be born prematurely, but that it didn't necessarily mean something was wrong. They could be born tiny, but they could also have complications. Still, I remained hopeful. I was a father now—I had to be strong. "Mr. Frans, unfortunately, you won't be able to go inside. But you can see your daughter through the window," the doctor explained, pointing toward a small infant lying on the right side of the room. "She weighs one kilo and eight hundred fifty grams, and she's forty-three centimeters long. A little fighter!" he added. I was overwhelmed with joy—I couldn't believe my eyes. My daughter was absolutely beautiful. The first thing I noticed was that her tiny nose looked just like Alice's. There were a few wisps of blonde hair on her head. I couldn't stop my tears. She was perfect. I could watch her forever.

Max never left my side. I was grateful he was here with me. I felt awful, so it was Max who went to the other room to check on our daughter and make sure everything was okay. I was afraid to have this conversation with him, but I had to. "Max, we need to talk," I said, grabbing his hand and kissing it lightly. "I'm listening, my love," he replied. I knew he had already noticed the sadness on my face. "Max, I love you more than life itself. You, Adam, and Lidia. But you know how much our happiness brings misfortune…" I started, but he cut me off, covering my mouth with his hand. "Please, don't say anything. This is all my fault. I failed to protect you. It won't happen again. I would die if anything happened to you," he insisted.

"This isn't your fault! I don't even want to think about what would have happened if you weren't there. You saved Adam's life. Max, this is not your fault. If we hadn't fought so hard to be together, none of this would have happened. We should never have started this, and we definitely shouldn't have kept going. Do you understand? This is my fault. I bring nothing but trouble upon us, and it's never going to stop", I said, my voice rising.

"Alice, I will never leave you. If you're trying to tell me that we shouldn't be together, that is the biggest nonsense I have ever heard. We love each other, we are getting married, and we are a family," Max countered. "I don't want to live in a world where Olaf still exists. He will never give up. He will destroy me and everyone I love," I added. "My love, you were never his property! You are not a prisoner of that man. How many times have I told you that I will endure anything? That I will be by your side no matter what happens? You are my love. The mother of my child." Max had also raised his voice.

Our conversation lasted a few minutes, but we kept coming back to it hundreds of times. I didn't know what we should do, but I couldn't let my family suffer any longer. I wanted to die. It was the first time in my life that I had such dark thoughts. Max had been sick, and then this happened. What was I supposed to do? Whenever we weren't arguing about our future, we talked about our little girl. Today was the day they would finally bring her to me. I was overjoyed. When the nurse rolled a small cart into my room, I felt like I was about to jump out of bed. I had never been so excited! When Adam was born, I had been just as happy, but I had also been scared. I hadn't been ready for pregnancy back then, but it had happened anyway. Our daughter had golden-white hair. She didn't have much of it yet, but I noticed it immediately—it reminded me of Max's.

I imagined her growing up, and me braiding her pigtails one day. Her eyes were still dark for now, but I could already see that they had taken the shape of Max's, which was wonderful news. I was so happy that she looked like him. To me, he was the most handsome man on earth. So, of course, our daughter would be beautiful, there was no other possibility. I kissed her tiny hands, ears, and feet endlessly. Max sat beside me on the bed, and together we gazed at this tiny miracle we had created. It broke my heart that she had come into the world under such circumstances. But I knew she could not have been more loved than she was now, here, with us. She was born out of our beautiful love. I couldn't wait to go home, but I knew we still had a long road of medical checkups ahead of us. Max also needed time to fully recover. I knew he would be fine. I was much more worried about our little girl, about Adam and how he would cope with everything.

But I never forgot about Max. He had shielded my child with his own body. I knew he would do it again if he had to. He wouldn't just give his life for me, but also for my child. He was a wonderful man. That's why I loved him so much. "What now?" I asked Max. "What do you mean, my love?" he replied, stroking little Lidia's hand. "I mean, what do we do now? About Olaf?" I continued. "We do nothing. We will be happy. Actually, I had an idea," Max said, now stroking my hand as well. "I'm listening," I said.

"I was thinking about moving. Buying a house outside the city. Something as charming as this one. Starting fresh," Max suggested. "But honey, you love our house! Can you really imagine living somewhere else?" I asked. "Alice, I don't want this neighborhood and this house to be associated with only bad memories. Yes, we had wonderful moments here. We fell in love. We moved in together. But this place still carries too much darkness with it," Max explained. "Do you think we can just throw ourselves into such a big change?" I asked hesitantly. "We can handle anything!" he said, kissing my forehead.

After two weeks, we were finally able to return home. Max was still complaining about pain in his stomach, but the doctor reassured us that it was nothing serious. It would take some time for him to recover fully. I was hopeful. On the way home, we talked about the changes we wanted to make in our lives. We planned to buy a house outside the city with a large plot of land, and I wanted to rent a space for my little flower shop. A job for me in our new place was still a distant plan, but we could already start making decisions together. Max didn't want to change his job, not only because of his salary but also because he genuinely liked his work. He decided he would only change offices to one closer to our new home but remain with the same company. There was so much to discuss that I couldn't process everything at once.

Max's phone rang. "Hello? Yes, speaking", Max answered, listening carefully to the person on the other end. "Yes, yes... That's great! Thank you very much!" he said, ending the call. "What happened?" I noticed a huge smile spreading across his face. "Baby, they locked him up! They really locked him up! Can you believe it? He got a life sentence!" Max said, hitting the steering wheel twice in excitement before grabbing my hand and kissing it. "No way! Really? That's amazing news!" I cheered, but then an image of my son flashed before my eyes. How much would I have to go through to explain all of this to him one day?

When we arrived home, Adam and Matilda were waiting for us at the door. My son's face was lit up with such a big smile—I had never seen him so euphoric before. Max carried Lidia's baby carrier inside and placed it gently on the hallway floor before closing the door behind him. Little Adam was overjoyed, inspecting his baby sister from every angle. He was so sweet and loving that I could hardly believe my eyes. He carefully covered her tiny legs with a blanket and took her little hand in his, stroking it gently.

Matilda couldn't resist and followed Adam's lead. After a while, she finally stood up and threw her arms around both of us. "Welcome home, my dear ones. It's so good to see you. I heard the news too. You're safe now. I was so worried about you!" she whispered into our ears before slowly pulling away. That entire evening, we spent cuddling Adam and staring at little Lidia. It was one of the happiest moments of my life. I sat in my favorite armchair, surrounded by my whole world. It was perfect. I wanted the moment to last forever.

Around eight o'clock, we heard Max's phone ringing again. "Hello? Yes, this is Max," he answered. "What? That's impossible", he added, rubbing his forehead and pushing back a strand of his hair. "Thank you, Doctor. See you tomorrow." His face turned pale. "My love. What happened?" I carefully laid Adam and Lidia down, as they had both fallen asleep in my arms. "My doctor called. I need to go to the hospital tomorrow," Max said, running his fingers through his hair and exhaling deeply. "Max, talk to me!" I shouted; my voice filled with fear. "It's spread," he whispered.

My world shattered into a million pieces again. Just when I thought everything would finally be okay. Once again, I could lose him. Even though we didn't know the full details yet, just the thought of it terrified me. I couldn't lose this life, our life together. Max threw his arms around me and broke down in tears. "My love, I love you," he whispered, kissing my forehead and pulling me even closer. "Max, I love you too. I will always love you."

The End.

www.ingramcontent.com/pod-product-compliance
Lightning Source LLC
Chambersburg PA
CBHW072006170626
46813CB00005B/2036